# THE UNDERSTORY

# THE
# UNDERSTORY

## Saneh Sangsuk

Translated from the Thai
by Mui Poopoksakul

DEEP VELLUM PUBLISHING
DALLAS, TEXAS

Deep Vellum Publishing
3000 Commerce Street, Dallas, Texas 75226
deepvellum.org · @deepvellum

Deep Vellum is a 501c3 nonprofit literary arts organization
founded in 2013 with the mission to bring
the world into conversation through literature.

Support for this publication has been provided in part by the National Endowment for the
Arts, the Texas Commission on the Arts, the City of Dallas Office of Arts and Culture, the
PEN/Heim Translation Fund, and the George and Fay Young Foundation.

ISBNs: 978-1-64605-275-2 (paperback) | 978-1-64605-296-7 (ebook)

LIBRARY OF CONGRESS CATALOGING-IN-PUBLICATION DATA

Names: Saneh Sangsuk, author. | Poopoksakul, Mui, translator.
Title: The understory / Saneh Sangsuk ; translated from the Thai by Mui
  Poopoksakul.
Other titles: Čhao kārakēt. English
Description: Dallas, Texas : Deep Vellum Publishing, 2024.
Identifiers: LCCN 2023039964 (print) | LCCN 2023039965 (ebook) | ISBN
  9781646052752 (trade paperback) | ISBN 9781646052967 (ebook)
Subjects: LCGFT: Novels.
Classification: LCC PL4209.D28 C4713 2024 (print) | LCC PL4209.D28
  (ebook) | DDC 895.9/134--dc23/eng/20231122
LC record available at https://lccn.loc.gov/2023039964
LC ebook record available at https://lccn.loc.gov/2023039965

Front Cover Design by Emily Mahon
Interior Layout and Typesetting by KGT

PRINTED IN THE UNITED STATES OF AMERICA

To the valiant souls of my maternal great-grandparents
and my father's mother:
the source of many wondrous tales.

Literature has nine flavors:

| | |
|---|---|
| *Sringara* | the taste of which is love |
| *Raudra* | the taste of which is anger |
| *Veera* | the taste of which is courage |
| *Bibhatsa* | the taste of which is disgust |
| *Hasya* | the taste of which is laughter |
| *Karuṇa* | the taste of which is pity and compassion |
| *Adbhuta* | the taste of which is amazement |
| *Bhayanaka* | the taste of which is fear |
| *Shanta* | the taste of which is peace |

—*The Rasavahini*

from the Thai edition translated by Saeng Monvitoon

right at their front steps and seized the chance to fish right in their own yards, and everybody caught copious amounts of different kinds of fish, which they smoked or cured with salt or fermented and kept in jars large and small. But the paddy crops had suffered no small degree of damage. The surviving rice plants came up tall and stringy like climbers, and when they sprouted ears, they were populated by small, deflated grains rather than the usual, plump ones, and all that season, there wasn't a child in Praeknamdang who got to eat any pandan rice pudding at all, however much they begged their mothers or grandmothers to make them some. It was the animals who first sensed the deluge and the calamity it would bring. Bees built their hives only on high-up branches; baya weavers too built their nests on high-up branches; serpents and other such creatures, both poisonous and not, flocked to hillocks or rises or tall trees; and green tree ants grew wings and began to fly about, relocating their nests to areas they thought beyond the flood's reach. The people of Praeknamdang paid heed to the animals and relayed what they were seeing to one another, to their children and grandchildren, and could foresee the situation they were about to face, the hardships they would have to bear and the struggles that were in store for them. It was a night near the end of December in 2510 BE, or 1967 CE, and the tam kwan khao ceremonies for the Goddess of Rice had come and gone, this time mirthless occasions without the usual fanfare, even subdued like a funeral, but the harvest season hadn't yet arrived. For the people of Praeknamdang, it was a period of rest. Everyone among them was somber, in despair and miserable, weighed down by all the problems such as there were. All the physical and mental effort that they had dedicated to their land during the planting season would, it was now clear, prove practically pointless. Even the children were

*Road Behind the House of Golden Sand.*" It was the year the only son of Kraam Kichagood, the latter the owner of a large herd of cattle and Praeknamdang's village chief, was preparing to go and continue his education in town, which meant he had better opportunities in life than the other children in Praeknamdang of his age group, nearly all of whom received only a third-grade education. It was a year when the great lady Ms. Prayong Sisan-ampai still taught at the local Praeknamdang Temple School, still harbored big hopes and big dreams for the children of Praeknamdang, her pupils, when she imagined their futures: that when they grew up, they would possess fulgent and beautiful spirits, like the one Ms. Prayong herself had, and entertain big hopes and big dreams, like she herself did, and never in their lives allow themselves to become creatures of despair, no matter how much and how often misery would be theirs to endure. It was the year the Venerable Father Tien Thammapanyo, or Luang Paw Tien, the abbot of Praeknamdang Temple, turned ninety-three years old, and was seventy-three years into his monkhood, and though his body was ancient and he suffered because of his asthma and arthritis, he remained vital enough to walk his alms route into the village nearly every day, the round-trip distance just shy of seven kilometers, and Kamin, his big ox who was tame as a dog, still tagged along right behind him and ate for his meals whatever food Luang Paw Tien received as alms, ate not only bananas, sugarcane, watermelon, and oranges and such, but everything, indiscriminately, be it curry over rice or rice with salt-cured fish or sweets, as long as it was Luang Paw Tien who hand-fed the food to him, the ox being unwilling to accept food from anyone else's hand, being that he had once been severely injured when he had stumbled in a wua lan race, and for that he had been slated for slaughter, but Luang Paw Tien had, on an alms round, any education who, until the moment he was gasping for his final breath, remained faithful to communist ideology in its pure form as evidenced by the fact that after being gunned down, he still strained to gather the last bits of his remaining strength to shout out "Long live the Communist Party of Thailand!"; he died without having the faintest idea that the bullet that punctured his abdomen and blew through his vertebrae was an M16 bullet fired by the hands of Wonrung Teptaro, his own dear friend—the two of them had been born in the same year, and growing up, they used to strip naked and cannonball themselves into the water together, and spin tops together, and used to wrestle and fistfight each other, and used to fall out only to reconcile and deepen their friendship, and used to walk together from the village to their school, the Praeknamdang Temple School, in the morning and walk back together in the afternoon, and during one lunch break had snuck into the taithun beneath the temple's living quarters and stolen bantam chicken eggs and had been caught red-handed by Luang Paw Tien and been flogged for it, and in the third grade had had their palms slapped three times each by Ms. Prayong because neither of them could read the word "atmosphere"; he was shot and killed without having the faintest idea that his death was at the hands of Wonrung Teptaro, who had dropped out of school after the fourth grade and worked the rice fields and had taken up boxing as a side gig, using Wonrung S. Damnerngasem as his ring name, and had even fought in big-time, professional rings like Lumpini and Rajadamnern, but ultimately hadn't been able to make much of himself in boxing and had drifted or been dragged along by others until he joined the Volunteer Defense Corps and was sent to be stationed in a "reddish" zone in Kui Buri District, where he ultimately chanced upon the opportunity to kill his own dear friend like something out of a and when Luang Paw Tien's body was laid inside a coffin and brought to the funeral pavilion for merit rites, Kamin followed him there and lay guarding his casket, urinating there and defecating there, refusing to leave his side no matter how the monks and novices tried to chase him away, and Kamin himself turned into an aged bull, skinny to the point that the entire rack of his ribs was visible, weeping to the point that tears came out not in drops but in streams, his long, crescent horns fell off one after the other, while his hide was dry and matted and unkempt, and fifteen days after Luang Paw Tien's passing, Kamin followed him in death. It was fifteen years before Kraam Kichagood would reappear in Praeknamdang, now as a bhikkhu, centered and serene, a monk seasoned in leading the vagabond life of tudong and an expert in the practice of Vipassana Kammatthana, and would try to found a Vipassana meditation center at Praeknamdang Temple, to teach what he claimed was Luang Pu Man Puritatto's method of Vipassana Kammatthana, even as he declined to attend to the villagers' suffering, which was caused by their destitution, refusing to give the villagers advice on how to better go about making their living, even though back when he was a layman, he had kept fish ponds and had raised pigs and ducks and chickens and had farmed rice and grown different crops and had been the owner of a large herd of a local breed of cattle, the successes of which had made him into a man of wealth, into a quintessential country gentleman; refusing to discuss anything having to do with earthly pursuits indeed, his excuse being that those weren't pursuits that would extinguish misery, and all he would do was coax, and sometimes outright push, people into taking up the practice of dharma, even though in his heart he must have realized full well that the inhabitants of Praeknamdang were bankrupt croppers facing death by

Praeknamdang, refusing to set down roots there, saying he was going to return to Bangkok, saying he was by nature a chaser of dreams and pursuer of imagination, that he had "literary duties," that he would never return to Praeknamdang ever again, and though he was sorry he could not stay with the people of Praeknamdang while they faced the final act of their tragedy, the role of the hero who would save Praeknamdang was not a role that should be given to him but should be played by somebody else, and after floating through the village and fields of his birth and boyhood for three days and three nights like a ghost that had died of unnatural causes, he left Praeknamdang without a trace, just as he had shown up—*that son of a bitch,* people said. But on that cold winter night, in 2510 BE, the children of Praeknamdang were still all present: Choob, Chid, Prai, Pun, Peug, Gloy, Wonrung, Wonram and Ruang and Prae and Kraam Kichagood's only son. Some of them were sitting, some lying down on cowhide rugs with a layer of hay spread on top for extra cushioning. Each wore many layers of shabby clothes to shield them from the cold; some of these garments were comically short on them, having already seen them through two or three winters—children grow so fast—while some of the clothes the children were swimming in, because they were hand-me-downs from their parents or older siblings. The skin on the children's arms and legs felt tight and chapped from the cold, and was starting to flake, and their lips were starting to feel tight and to become chapped as well, and all of the children developed a shared problem, which was that the cold constantly made them feel like they had to pee, and the girls, who had to lift up their sarongs or peel down their pants in the process of squatting down to relieve themselves, would whisper to one another afterward how every time they went to pee, their butts froze and their coochies froze. As gathered here seeking the simple joy of chatting quietly with one another and listening quietly to one another. They rarely drank anything intoxicating, and never on nights when Luang Paw Tien was part of the group; they mostly drank bael juice or medlar tea or jasmine tea. These nightly gatherings would commence after the last downpours of the monsoon season and would cease when the rice plants in the paddy fields showed ears golden enough to harvest. Time and time again, they sat there like that until dawn, and Luang Paw Tien would stay there all night, too, and then take his breakfast there. The adults, sitting placidly by the fire, seemed lifeless compared to the children, who on these nights would make full use of the blaze by grilling chicken eggs or straw mushrooms or roasting taro or sweet potatoes or corn. The children never failed to find something to grill or roast. Even on meager nights, they still managed to come up with Silver Bluggoe bananas or overripe Namwah bananas to cook in the fire and share among themselves. They could always find *something*: even sugarcane or young coconuts or bamboo shoots weren't to be overlooked. On nights when the pickings were slim, the children persevered and went about collecting tamarind seeds so they would have something to toast and crunch in their mouths for the fun of it, and after they were finished with their snacks, they would pile themselves together like a bunch of puppies, and after horsing around, after some taunting and teasing and some fighting, lots of the children would doze off, and lie quiet and still. But there were always some that stayed awake and sat quietly or lay quietly listening to the adults' conversation, and the winter breeze would carry on sweeping through the fields. There was a melancholy to the stillness of their surroundings, and the village looked fragile against that vast, lonely landscape. It looked like something meaningless, whenever Pone Kingpetch or Chartchai Chionoi took to the ring and the match was broadcast live on the radio, he would listen intently, cheering loudly for them, the sentiment behind his support blatantly nationalist. He would listen to the matches with his Kamin and throw his hardest punches and jabs at the ox's neck or hump, or its body, pretending that Kamin was Pone's or Chartchai's foreign opponent. But Kamin didn't mind, he barely felt a thing, and just lay there, drowsy-eyed and burping, chomping on his cud. All in all, Luang Paw Tien wasn't your *comme il faut* sort of monk. The folks in Praeknamdang were by now used to the sight of him walking or running in the paddy fields next to the temple in only his sabong and angsa, and with a towel wrapped around his head while helping the village boys fly their star- or diamond-shaped kites, or of him seated on the ground, surrounded by a group of boys, making spinning tops out of guava wood to give out to them, or of him seated on the ground, surrounded by a group of girls, teaching them how to do simple weaving with bamboo strips or coconut or palm fronds; his technique in this particular craft was fairly limited, all he could show them how to make were the very basic chalom baskets, or mobile pieces in the shape of barb fish, or takraw balls, but he was happy to impart what knowledge he had. To the serious-minded adults, he was a teller of tall tales who breached the precept concerning monks and untruthful speech, but to the children, he was a trove of magical stories. Most people were able to look past his minor solecisms. He could be a yeller, but he was kind: he was liable to give anybody a talking-to or even a tongue-lashing, and that was fine, and if someone really made his blood boil, he would whack them with his famous walking stick—but all this was accepted as his way of showing his care and concern, and simply part of putting an ox to work on a Buddhist holy day, he would go and scold them. For all of these reasons, everybody loved and respected him. Never had he divulged to anyone how, because he was such an ardent fan of the literary program on the radio, he secretly harbored ambitions of becoming a writer himself, and he spent his free time, which he had plenty of, scribbling down episode upon episode of his life story, some of which made for discrete little tales in and of themselves, others of which were yet incomplete fragments, but when he read over these writings later, without exception he found them to be either nonsense, total malarkey, or not colorful and flavorful enough, and though all of them were true stories, they didn't seem believable, and then he would agonize and feel guilty and turn to praying for long stretches at a time, ashamed to have involved himself in something that was outside of a bhikkhu's duties, ashamed when thinking about how if Lord Buddha were to learn of his transgression, the good Lord would chide him for it. But after a period of remorse, he would feel the itch to write again, or feel the itch to relate the stories in his head to other people again. The more mature and sensible villagers, the practical-minded and serious ones, weren't particularly interested in his stories; they dismissed them as an old man's ramblings. But the children of Praeknamdang always wanted to hear his tales. He was now ninety-three years old and seventy-three years into his monkhood, and even though, all in all, he was still strong and in good health and liked to put on a show to prove as much, what he had been keeping to himself was that, over the past four or five years, his once superior eyesight had declined and his tongue had begun to grow dull to flavor; that sometimes he couldn't hear very well, and during conversations, he relied on lipreading rather than listening to his interlocutor's words; that at the piece of the earth where once upon a time our blessed Lord Buddha had stamped his holy footprints," an adventure during which he wandered alone through a wilderness of jungles and mountains and caverns and caves, a true tudong pilgrimage strictly in keeping with the holy austerity practice of dhutanga as prescribed by Lord Buddha twenty-five centuries ago. There and back, the journey took him a whole fifteen years, during which time he stopped along the route whenever he found a cave or a monastery or a temple or any kind of place serene enough for meditation and prayers, and cloistered himself for the three rainy months of each Buddhist Lent in abandoned temples, and stayed for long periods at a time in cemeteries, and let himself stray off course several times and got lost on several occasions, along the way learning the languages of the Karen, Mon, Bru, Wa, and Khmu peoples and a number of other local languages of Burma and India as well, though none to the point where his knowledge of them was profound or his command firm—he could only answer simple questions, could only carry on a basic conversation: Where are you from? Where are you going? Have you eaten? Are there any Buddhist communities or Buddhist temples in this area? He trod straight west to Burma, and from there trod straight north to India, and there had had to keep his sadness confined within him when he discovered that in the land of Buddha's time on earth, the number of Buddhists was smaller than small; that now all that remained of the sacred bodhi tree where Lord Buddha had attained enlightenment was a fourth-generation sucker shoot, rather than the grand tree of magnificent beauty like he had imagined; that now the Niranjana River had nearly completely dried up to nothing more than a puny runnel, dirty and full of weeds and shrubs, and had become a feeding ground for herds of cows and goats and a place where the locals, who were not adherents of Buddhism, came to relieve themselves; that the Gijjhakuta did not loom over the landscape like an Olympian mountain, but was a mere hill, unimpressive in size and height, and a bare and bald-looking one at that; and he found that of the pilgrims who made their way to the four holy sites, most were Burmese or Sri Lankans, with hardly any Thais among them, whether monks or layfolk, and all of this broke his heart. The people of Praeknamdang, meanwhile, had believed him dead, and every year on the New Year's holiday of Songkran, they made offerings at the temple, dedicating the benefit to his soul, and when he returned from his odyssey, they needed to think long and hard before it dawned on them that the bhikkhu with the big, tall, sturdy build whose cumbersome feet were covered in cuts both old and fresh, whose robe and sabong had been worn ragged and stank of mildew, whose large, dark eyes housed a look at once startled, sad, and faraway, was none other than he. Praeknamdang had changed so much that he hardly recognized it. The untouched jungle land had been wiped out because of forest concessions. The local stream had become deeper and wider than it used to be, and branches upon branches had been dug off of it. Areas that had once been forest land now had owners and had been cleared into planting fields, and the people, both the original inhabitants and the newcomers, no longer lived off the jungle but were farmers and orchardists. He often said that he had not been present to bear witness to the obliteration of the jungle, but it was he who was the last remaining witness to a time when all around Praeknamdang was jungle, everywhere you looked; a time when human settlements had been something foreign, and their accompanying fields, orchards, farms, and paddies foreign land. He would often begin his stories by reminding his listeners of how much had changed, and in just one lifetime. Anytime he began a story, any story at all, it always looked like he was telling it to the children specifically—he liked to see the smiles on their faces, liked their dramatic reactions when they were scared or when they were bewildered, and he hardly registered the adults' presence at all. It wasn't something he did consciously, though deep down he knew well the adults were too passive in spirit, too tainted, too bruised, and had endured too much despair and too much misery, "that their hearts were as calloused and deadened as heels that had weathered too much," and it was the children who were truly eager to listen to his tales. Prae Anchan, Put Anchan's daughter, a girl of ten who had large eyes, tangled sun-fried hair, and a dark scar at the outer corner of her left eye, and who always surprised people with her beautiful penmanship and could read and do arithmetic better than the other children her age and was first in her class every time, was pulled aside by Ms. Prayong Sisan-ampai and given instructions to remember and write down every one of the stories told to them by Luang Paw Tien. This girl, Prae, excelled at composition, and she had put other stories down on paper too, ones that Ms. Prayong had not assigned to her. These were entries about her rainbow sightings, in which she noted the date, time, and her location when she spotted the rainbow, the duration of the rainbow's visibility, and even details about what she was doing and with whom, or if she was alone at the time of each observance and which trees were in bloom and which birds were chirping. Her compositions recording Luang Paw Tien's stories and those documenting her rainbow sightings (which Ms. Prayong later discovered and thought showed great promise) were regularly brought out and read aloud in the afternoon at school in Thai class.

an inch. All around him spread the jungle, moonlit and filled with comfortless silence, replete with danger and mystery, every corner and nook haunted by creatures of every shape and size, some natural and some beyond nature. But in that moment, nothing mattered but the screams of the wild elephants, whose ring was tightening around him. The way they had deployed themselves and encircled him made known their displeasure, their ire, their suspicion, their uncertainty, as well as their curiosity in having stumbled upon a shaven-headed human being, draped in the color of dirt, on his knees, a vague silhouette within a sorry little tent canopy also the color of dirt, the fabric of which was as threadbare as could be, full of holes and patches, this human a stranger in their empire, and all of them, much vexed, stomped back and forth in front of his glot, odd noises coming from their mouths and trunks as if they were conferring with one another, or trying either to incite or dissuade one another. The ones that had advanced closer to his canopy were all enormous creatures, both bulls and cows, each nine or ten cubits in height, at once splendid and hideous and ill-tempered in their expressions; they were like boulders on the move, their thick, coarse skin marked with deep crisscrossed lines forming odd geometric shapes, their legs as thick as tree trunks, and their tusks (if they had tusks) were elegant, white arcs rising to their tips, and even as his heart pounded in fright, he still found himself marveling at the fact that this herd of wild elephants had a female leader: her body black and as colossal as a giant's, immeasurably old, ears fanned all the way taut, trunk held aloft and swinging side to side, she looked like a creature from another world. All the other elephants in the herd kept their eyes on their matriarch, and their ears perked, waiting for a signal from her: retreat, sidestep, or attack. The other elephants were all her children helped ensure its continued survival, but their various repeated offenses had proved too much to tolerate, and in the end, though her love was boundless, her patience had a limit. She could not continue to forgive them, and her memories of those losses made her struggle to sleep, made her suffer nightmares and sometimes whimper out in her slumber, and one or another of the remaining elephants would console her exactly the way a human child or grandchild would console their elderly mother or grandmother: "You shouldn't torture yourself over Papa. It's time you let him go. His fate is beyond our fixing," or, "Don't be sad about Grandpa, Grandma. His soul's probably gone to a better place," or, "Grandma, why would you miss that rogue older brother of mine? A no-good elephant like him! He knew full well what he did was wrong, and yet he went and did it anyway," and he, Luang Paw Tien, fixed his eyes on the grande dame elephant until his spirit and hers melded into one, and he was able to apprehend the love and magnanimity within her, absorb her bitter memories and make them his own, comprehend the necessity behind her actions, and all he could do was pray for her and say quietly to her, "Your earthly suffering will probably soon be over. You're going to be reincarnated as a woman, and whatever your position in life, I'm confident you'll be a great lady, a heroine." But then he saw that, contrary to his anticipation, the old matriarch reacted by thrusting her trunk even higher, spreading her ears even farther out, and unleashing a high-pitched battle cry, which made the other elephants unleash high-pitched battle cries of their own, joining her in a collective fanfare, and the young tudong monk felt a chill crawling down his spine and noticed cold sweat running over his hairless brows into his eyes and his eyes stinging from it, and he faltered on his words as he prayed, "*Buddham saranam gacchami. Dhammam saranam gacchami.*

*Sangham saranam gacchami,"* round and round again and uttered words of apology for having been insolent enough to inconvenience this clan of ancient creatures, who were endowed with intelligence and elegance, and whose spirits carried within them the mysterious and the miraculous; but later on uttered words of acceptance, of being at peace with his fate, all the while attempting to communicate with the wild elephants in the crude language of humans, which was utterly inappropriate and inadequate to convey his sincerity: "If in any previous life of mine, I've given you reason to bear a grudge against me and you wish to destroy me now, it's up to you to do as you wish. I'm not attached to my life, and I forgive you your karma. I'm merely on a journey to pay respect to the footprints of the Blessed Lord who once led his holy life in the faraway land of Jambudvipa, he who was the supreme promulgator of dharma. *Buddham saranam gacchami.*" His words and the prayers were all jumbled together; sometimes they were spoken through his lips, in a loud though shaky voice, sometimes they echoed only within the confines of his head. So terrified was he, and in such depths of despair, that he felt it was time for him to yield to his fate, and the despair was so deep that it drove him—so he admitted to his listeners around the fire—to such delusions that he thought he heard the elephants' footsteps charging in, heard their high-pitched din approaching nearer, and saw an elephant's huge wrinkly trunk, which, even more magical than a human hand, could move any degree in any direction, wind itself around his shabby little glot, tear it off the tree and hurl it away in anger, and that same trunk, now a hand of the Lord of Death, hooked him and wrapped itself around him and flung him high up into the air, whence his body dropped in free fall, but before it landed on the ground, it was pierced through, midair, by a big, long, pointed tusk, which had beasts with its ancient matriarch had the ability to strike the kind of fear that makes one lose one's wits, to provoke outright terror—but they could also inspire great reverence and were possessed of a wondrous beauty. The aged grandma's extensive clan, consisting of her children, grandchildren, great-grandchildren and great-great-grandchildren, was about to leave without harming him, and he sat there watching them depart, breathing more easily now, more fully into his lungs now, and with gratitude and compassion, he wished them good fortune, feeling glad that they had chosen not to sin, and glad for himself that in the end he was still alive, and as long as he was alive he would have hopes and dreams and have faith in a worthy duty he was to serve, whatever it may be or if it were to be more than one. So he nearly died from shock when out of nowhere, a snakelike trunk burst in through a hole in his canopy. It waved and fumbled about within, touching and sniffing his face, his neck, his chest, clearly inquisitive, but then lost interest in him, landing instead on an overripe bunch of wild bananas that stood beside his alms bowl and water canister, and swiftly reeling out the fruit. The trunk was a little one belonging to a little elephant at a naughty and nosy age, which, because of its dawdling, was straggling behind the herd; it was interested in nothing other than eating and playing, both in fantasy and in reality, taking itself as the center of the world, never mindful of what is right or wrong, never having regard for what is appropriate or inappropriate, and, just like a child, completely oblivious to all the dangers of the world. He, Luang Paw Tien, poked his face out of his canopy and saw the elephant calf busy maneuvering its trunk to pick up one of the overripe bananas, which had broken off from the bunch and fallen onto the ground, and popping it in its mouth, gleeful, greedy, giddy. Standing right nearby was its mother, who watched her young with a mixture of annoyance and endearment; with her trunk, she lightly spanked the calf on its back, exacting a flabby punishment—in that, she was no different from mothers everywhere who love and spoil their children too much. She didn't slap it hard enough to hurt it, but Grandma Senior, their matriarch, had deliberated and her decision had been for them to leave the bald bhikkhu alone, and the other elders of the herd had concurred, that no member of the herd was to disturb the bald bhikkhu, and thus the mother elephant had to been seen to teach her calf a lesson. Close to the pair stood another elephant cow, who watched the two of them with a stern look on her face and eyes that said *tsk-tsk*. No doubt this other female was the calf's second mother, the one who had been by the first mother's side, taking care of her, helping her, and giving her encouragement when she was heavily pregnant, and while she was birthing the calf, and this second mother took a big part in rearing the calf and protecting it from danger. She had nearly as much claim over the calf as the first mother did, and she stood ready to assert her claim when it came to doling out either rewards or punishments. The calf was growing up loved almost the same by its two mothers (such arrangements existed at least back when there was still jungle everywhere and elephants were left alone to live their lives according to their natural social order), and the second mother would step up and assume the role of first mother were the first mother to die or were fate to separate her from the herd. Not far from the two mothers, at the rear of the herd's caravan, there also stood a bull elephant, a big, strapping male in his prime, dark in color and intimidating, who had been impatiently observing this little episode with displeasure, until he finally marched straight up to the calf and gave it one good, hard lash on its back with his trunk. The calf still managed to nab itself another banana as it ran after the *hoarse, and his eyes welled up.* The children all played their part to help fill in the gaps until they were satisfied that the story was whole and to cut out anything superfluous until they were satisfied that the story was polished. Each of them was determined to safeguard the phrasing, forms, and flow of Luang Paw Tien's original stories, all of them insisting to Prae Anchan, the girl they knew had been expressly assigned the task, that she must record all of it faithfully so they would have it preserved in writing. All of this role-playing and impersonation the children did without telling Luang Paw Tien or any of the adults, because they feared Luang Paw Tien wouldn't understand, feared that if he were to catch wind of it he might become self-conscious and refuse to ever tell them another story again, however much they might beg and plead, and he might say something like, "Since you lot can tell my stories so expertly on your own, why should I waste my time?" But in reality, Luang Paw Tien loved to tell his tales, and had an endless number of them. Some of his tales were funny, some sad, some spooky; and often they were full of magic spells and supernatural powers. Nearly all of them were meant as frivolous entertainment and nothing more, and nearly none had a moral. The story about his close call with the herd of wild elephants: the children had heard it before and wanted to hear it again. The story about the time early in his days as a tudong monk when, on one cold winter night, a king cobra the length of twelve forearms slithered in and slept next to him: the children had heard that one before, too, and wanted to hear it again. The story about the time during one of his wanderings when he ventured into a secluded mountain range far away to the west and came upon a large cave full of stalactites and stalagmites in unusual shapes and colors, no two the same, and it was cold and damp and silent, which he found conducive to meditation and prayers, and the cave turned out to be full of gems and jewels and gold ornaments, surely a treasure trove belonging to one provincial ruler or another or one monarch or another, who had been defeated in battle or had a disaster befall him, forcing him to flee, and hide his riches; and he might have killed somebody, perhaps a courtier or a slave, so that the soul of the dead would guard and protect the trove, all of which might have happened in a bygone era, back when there were still local lords and wars, and in that cave Luang Paw Tien discovered the skeletons of four tudong monks, two of them long dead, two only recently so, their remains dressed in worn, torn, and tattered monk's robes, and all four of their alms bowls were filled to the brim with gems and jewels, suggesting that in that silent cave they had fallen prey to avarice, forgetting that their chosen life was the life of beggars, and were killed by the soul guarding the treasure trove: that story, too, the children had heard before and wanted to hear again. The story about the time during one of his tudong adventures when he encountered an ascetic robed in white who was one hundred and fifty years old but could pass for a young man of twenty-five because he had drunk an elixir of life, and who, because he took a liking to Luang Paw Tien, offered to share some of his magic potion and even generously offered to give Luang Paw Tien the recipe, but Luang Paw Tien declined to take the elixir and declined to accept the recipe, because in his view to live a too protracted life was, in truth, a kind of sin: that one, too, the children had heard before and wanted to hear again. The story about the tiger that gobbled up a person, the one in which the victim's soul ended up possessing the tiger, occupying its body like the master of the house, an act which turned the tiger into a sming—a creature tiger in body but evil spirit in soul—and gave it the ability to shapeshift into human form, which it proceeded to do throughout the village day and night without the people having the heart or the courage to shoo or chase him away, but at the same time they didn't dare to approach and comfort him either, and when he died, the villagers constructed a shrine to him, so his unfortunate soul could have a resting place, and from generation to generation they all worshipped and honored him by visiting the shrine and joining their palms before them or even prostrating themselves on the ground; later on, when a railroad was to be cut across the site of the shrine, the people moved it away, and later on still, the land where the shrine sat was laid claim to, and the new landowner, wanting to make farmland of it, cleared the plot and the shrine was razed with it; in subsequent eras, the memory faded of how once upon a time there had lived a hero who had transformed himself into a tiger to fight a tiger, and whenever people heard somebody tell the story, they would smile wryly and say it was all nonsense: that story, too, the children had heard before and yet wanted to hear again. The story about the crocodile hunter whose blunder caused him to be bitten by a crocodile, inflicting a grave wound requiring him to convalesce at home for more than a month, and who lost his mind because lounges upon lounges of house lizards stationed themselves at his side, waiting to lick the blood and pus from the bite wound, and when shooed away, they simply ran and took refuge in nooks and corners, which human homes are full of, and where lizards can easily and comfortably shelter themselves, and before long they inevitably reemerged, intent on eating the blood and pus from the wound again, and even when the invalid lay inside a mosquito net, they still came and congregated around the net, and they were joined by skinks, and tokay geckos, and all of them made little noises taunting him, tormenting him, eventually driving the crocodile hunter to madness because house lizards and

44

suddenly sat up. Those in their cohort who were still asleep were jolted awake; those still groggy were tickled at the waist, which made them jump, their eyes instantly alert. The children's faces were grubby and grimy, their clothes were grubby and grimy, but their eyes gleamed in the light of the fire. They observed Luang Paw Tien's every move, leaned their ears in to catch his every word. Although he was undoubtedly far ripened with age, everybody (other than Luang Paw Tien himself) was of the opinion that he was the most robust old man they had ever met. His hair, eyebrows, stubble, and even the little strings hanging out of his nose were all white, his face was creased and sagging, and he had spots and moles scattered all over his chest, back, shoulders, and the underside of his chin. He had a tall and solid build, which evinced that in his youth he must have been exceedingly strong, though all that remained on him now was wrinkled, drooping flesh. But he still had a full set of teeth, none of which wobbled at all, a testament to the benefit of drinking a tall glass of one's own urine a day, and his eyes still gleamed in the light of the fire, and his voice was still spry and cheery. He was their monk, and the most senior elder of Praeknamdang, which made all the people revere him, and the grandness of his heart made all of them love him. Everyone, even his fellow bhikkhus, forgave him his unmonkly peccadilloes, forgiving the fact that when he walked into the village, he didn't train his eyes restrainedly forward while looking no more than three steps ahead as he was supposed to do according to Buddhist commandments, but rather he let his eyes rove around, falling on this and that and looking much too far ahead. When a large tree on the temple's grounds sprang a wayward branch, he would grab an axe and climb up and prune it himself, instead of assigning the task to a novice or asking a villager to help. It wasn't only by the stream in front of the temple that he planted a SANCTUARY ZONE sign; he extended his sanctuary zone far, far out along the bank. Whenever one of the teachers at the local Praeknamdang Temple School had to miss a lesson, he would eagerly jump in and substitute. When dogs went at each other with their teeth, he had the maddening habit of getting in and breaking up the fight, frustrating the throng of spectators because they would never get to find out which dog would have won. When bulls went at each other with their horns, he did the same, again frustrating the spectators, who would never get to find out which bull would have won. When Praeknamdang held a celebration and a generator and a loudspeaker were brought in, he would go and force the disc jockey to play Toon Tongjai at the crack of dawn as a way of waking everybody up, and to play Phon Phirom's story songs about the Buddha's past lives at night as a way of sending people to bed (as for the period in between, any music could be selected and he wouldn't intervene). He couldn't refrain from meddling in the villagers' worldly pursuits, despite knowing the impropriety, and as a mediator of disputes, he had a stunningly high success rate, for while he did not know a single article of the law, he well understood the meaning of justice. But his great skill was as a storyteller, where he had a way of adapting his tone, manner, and voice to whatever the tale required from him. Presently, he held his head tilted back, viewing the sky, bright with moonlight and twinkling starlight; he spun his face toward the row of bamboo groves right as a koel bird within happened to caw out in its sleep; then he lowered his eyes and peered between the toddy palms on the horizon to the east, looking as if he was waiting to catch the gold and silver lights of dawn. The winter breeze continued to gently brush the trees, blowing steadily through the village. The later the hour, the quieter the sky, and the land beneath cooks noticed as much, and so they served him the same again the following day. But in those times, we didn't have refrigerators, we didn't have what they call "high technology in food preservation," so the shrimp was no longer fresh. When His Majesty ate the goong jom again, he took ill, suffered excruciating stomach pain, and died. His Great Departed Majesty also had a habit of chewing betel nut, and his teeth were black. So, when he was planning a visit to Europe, he became concerned about the matter and had to have his teeth polished. Do you know why he took a trip to Europe? A Western doctor had advised him to travel to Europe so he'd put some distance between himself and his bevy of queens, consorts and concubines and have something of a break from them—at least that's what people say. Regardless, he was a true paragon of monarchy, a paragon of man, even. There was one time when his son Krom Luang Chumphon Khet Udomsak, the Prince of Chumphon, was in an unappeasable fury—it was when the French captured the city of Chanthaburi. This particular prince, though he'd received a Western education, was keenly interested in spells and magic and in traditional medicine. He was a disciple of Luang Paw Suk of Makham Thao Temple and had followed the true course of study in occultism for real Siamese men. He was also a great devotee of Thai boxing and was a patron of all the ace boxers of the day. The prince not only kept the company of commoners but also counted ruffians among his followers and friends, of which he had many. When the French took Chanthaburi, he went to have an audience with his father, His Majesty the King, to seek His Majesty's permission to gather his men to fight the French. His Majesty forbade him, telling his son that his plan would be tantamount to using a twig to pry a log off the ground. When the French then took the city of Trat, he went to have another audience with His Majesty the King, again to seek His Majesty's permission to raise an army to take back the city. His Majesty forbade him for a second time: it would be like using a twig to pry a log. Krom Luang Chumphon left the meeting livid, and soon afterward had the word "Trat" tattooed in black ink on the left side of his chest. His dauntless troop of men then all had the word "Trat" tattooed on their chests as well—at least that's what people say. Krom Luang Chumphon has my love and respect because of that. Time was Siamese men would wield spells and magic as a matter of course; they learned the art to protect themselves as well as to demand and extract justice. It's an art that requires great mental strength. All occultists, without exception, are persons of great mental strength. In these things that people today, you listening now, probably see as silly and absurd, my faith is blind, it is unshakeable. Especially when magic is deployed as a force for good, my faith in it is absolutely unshakable—I'm wholly convinced of its power. But when magic is deployed as a force for evil, I scoff at it and regard it with contempt, I'm half believing, half disbelieving, because evil is in and of itself a fragile thing, while good is a thing of strength. Good is stronger even than death. Good people, people who are determined to do good deeds, are strong. They may be lowly, ordinary people, without power or wealth, but there's strength in them, whether they recognize it or not, and if they're truly good, nothing can destroy them. People who employ magic in the service of noble, righteous ends—those are the people who'll see their powers grow ever more potent. The occultist who transformed into a tiger in order to kill the local lord and thereby avenge his father was a great man because his actions spoke the essence of justice. The occultist who transformed into a tiger in order to fight the tiger that had shown up in his village and killed people in his community, to be wild water buffaloes and huge herds of bantengs—that's right, and even tapirs. There used to be apitong trees looming high over the rest of the forest and makhas and crape myrtles and takhians and tengs and red lauans. And there used to be water vines. If you were only a little thirsty, you'd cut yourself only a little one. Tremendously refreshing, utterly flavorless water would gush out, and if you were very thirsty, you'd cut yourself a very big one. Then you could drink your fill and still have some left to splash your face with or rinse off with, or cook a meal. Nowadays, I don't see them anymore, these water vines—they've been wiped out with the jungle. Bogs and swamps and marshes around here used to be teeming with crocodiles, big ones and small ones, and they could be seen soaking themselves in the mud or basking in the morning sun, and there'd be little grayish, blackish birds called crocodile birds bouncing within their wide-gaped mouths, picking out scraps of food. These days, all that's left are Bengal monitors and water lizards. The crocodile birds have vanished along with the crocodiles. In my mind's eye I can see them now: a large congregation of crocodiles lazing by the side of a swamp; with their thick, tough skin, coarse and lumpy and always coated in mud, they were the embodiment of hideousness, these creatures as old as time, parked among patches of blood lilies, which are such lissome, beautiful, delicate plants, with ravishing red blossoms that sway ever so subtly in dawn's whispering wind. And there used to be large fish aplenty: giant mudfish and striped snakeheads the size of legs, clown featherbacks the size of giant woks. Turtles and softshell turtles were commonplace. There were even small-headed softshell turtles as big as oxcarts, weighing a ton, easily, I reckon, truly gargantuan. It's a pity that none of you here are likely to have the chance to see those small-headed softshell turtles anymore. You palms, the canes twenty, thirty arm spans in length, twined all over tall trees. Hunters from elsewhere used to come and source rattan from here for their own use. They'd hack loose canes that were as thick as a person's thigh or calf, hack them near to the ground, and make their elephants drag them down. Elephants aren't exactly known for their faint hearts, but even *they* yowled, even *they* wanted to give up. They started down here, the rattans, but they reached all the way up there, all the way to the treetops. Oh, the jungle . . . I was born in the jungle, grew up in the jungle. In those days, people in Praeknamdang used to live off it. The jungle . . . so much of it was an enigma to me, so much beyond my comprehension, no matter how I tried to make sense of it. Take elephant boneyards, for example: I've never seen one, Old Man Junpa had never seen one either, but he said his father and his father's father used to speak of them. Or these things called kods. According to Old Man Junpa, inside giant, centuries-old termite mounds, sometimes you'll find these strange objects: these hard, white, roundish or ovalish nuggets with a smooth surface. They're not hardened soil, they're not stone, and they're not metal. People call them termite kods. If you get your hands on one and have a spellcaster put a charm on it, then you've got yourself a phenomenal talisman. These things are much coveted for their magical powers. Inside giant, centuries-old beehives, too, according to Old Man Junpa, sometimes you'll find similar objects: hard, white, roundish or ovalish nuggets with a smooth surface. They're not hardened beeswax, not stone, and not metal. They're bee kods instead of termite kods, also phenomenal talismans if you can get your hands on one. People in the old days believed in superstitions, and put their faith in talismans and magic charms, because these things gave them courage, and people were constantly surrounded by different dangers, in wartime and peacetime both.

As much as firepower and physical strength, they valued the mental strength derived from the practice of magic, not because they were fools but because they had to live with various limitations, being prisoners of their time. These termite kods and bee kods, I've never come across either. Even *I* am not old enough to have seen some of the things Old Man Junpa told me about. Crae birds, there's another example. Old Man Junpa said he'd seen them—they have the same size and build as crows, and are identical to crows in their character, meaning they're quick-eyed, clever little thieves. The only difference is they're not black, but dusty red from head to tail. These creatures, too, I've never laid eyes on. I thought I'd see some in Burma or India when I journeyed through those countries on my pilgrimage. I did look for them, but I didn't see any. Some people told me lots of them could still be found in Kandy—those who had trekked all the way to Kandy, Sri Lanka, to pay respect to the relic at the Temple of the Tooth said they saw many, many craes in the city. Old Man Junpa told me there used to be craes in Praeknamdang. Strange and sad . . . I've never had the opportunity to see one. Nor have I seen those wasps that live underground, in immense nests into which hapless animals, as well as sometimes hapless people, have fallen in and been overwhelmed and ultimately stung to death. These poor souls, animal or human, would, according to those who have seen it, try to stick a leg up, and in the blink of an eye, all that would be left of their leg was bone, clean-white. I've never seen it happen, and Old Man Junpa had never seen it happen either, but he said his father and his father's father used to speak of such occurrences. Once, I got stung by a banded hornet, the size of a little finger, with yellow and black stripes. It burned and hurt beyond bearing. It hurt down to the bone. It hurt to the point that my heart began palpitating. The hornet stung me tiger that got her. At the time of her passing, Old Man Junpa was away. He'd had to go and serve as a guide for the hunting expedition of some royal who'd come on a leisure hunt around the deep, dark woods of Sarahed District. By the time he returned, Glintoop had been dead nearly a year. I was told—and I don't know how much of it was true—that my sister had gone to play in the stream during the high-water season, and we had a big flood that year, too, and she'd drowned. As for me, at the time of my birth, Mae Duangbulan had named me Kwantien, "candle smoke." I only shortened it to Tien during the era of Field Marshal Plaek Phibunsongkhram's Cultural Revolution—the district chief paid me a visit and urged me to change it, so I did. But before that, everybody used to call me Kwantien, and I grew up as an only child. Mae Duangbulan, she wanted to farm, she wanted to take over the plot in the forest she'd already claimed and make rice fields of it. Before I could even crawl, she brought me along when she went out to the fields, and there she'd lay me on a cushion under a tree and tie my leg with a khao mah sash, tethering me to the trunk. She was fair-skinned, tall and strong, and, like most women of that era, she couldn't read or write. Unlike most women of that era, she didn't chew betel nut. She made such delicious gang liang and sang such beautiful lullabies—I still have those memories of her today. She was a guileless, reserved, melancholy woman dreaming of a stable life, and she had her heart set on converting forest land into fields. Old Man Junpa, however, had different ideas. Every day, when it came time to chop and dig and weed to ready the land for planting, he'd grab Ninlagaan, his trusty percussion rifle named after the onyx, and without fail disappear into the forest, returning hours later hauling a muntjac or a larger deer, or laden with gaur or banteng meat. On the surface, it might have appeared like he was lazy, but that wasn't it; he was simply reluctant to become a farmer, never quite ready to go against his heart. "I'm a grand, mighty river whose course is tough to change," he would say, almost as an excuse. In Praeknamdang in those days, as soon as you reached the bottom of your front steps, you were in the forest. There were only a few patches of farmland or field, and planting vegetables like greens and beans and such, and cultivating rice unirrigated, didn't work particularly well. Usually, elephants or bears or monkeys or boars or birds came and interfered. There was one year when Mae Duangbulan appeared set for an ample harvest. Seeing her rice plants sprout in large bouquets of golden yellow, she applied herself to preparations for a tam kwan khao ceremony: meticulously cooking dishes savory and sweet, stitching together a flag an arm span high in red and white, stringing a malai garland in seven colors and seven forearms long, all to be dedicated to the goddess of rice, Mae Posop. Just as she was about to reap the fruits of her labor, disaster struck: weaverbirds! From who knows where, ten thousand of them, I'd say, swooped down and devoured the crop in one go. They left her only with bare straws; she didn't even get a full sack of rice. Old Man Junpa, beyond pleased, rubbed it in her face: "See? What does farming get you?" But Mae Duangbulan refused to admit defeat. The following year, she planted new seeds and started farming all over again, on dry land. She dug holes, depositing four seeds into each of them— one for the beetles and the bugs in the soil, one for the crows, one for the monkeys and lemurs and such, and one for the person who did the planting. And her rice sprang up in lush, fluttering bunches, flourishing in the rain. Mae Duangbulan, pointing for me to look, said, "Behold Mae Posop's miracle!" Rice is a curious plant, when you think about it—it never fails to grow. It might stall if deprived of rain, but given rain, it'll grow in a hurry, and if weeds don't go meet Mae Duangbulan for her tam kwan khao ceremony. Her rice crop was just starting to show its yield. Mae Duangbulan had a red and white flag lodged into the ground, the pole reaching higher than her head, and next to it she'd placed a knee-high stand made of bamboo, onto which she then arranged foods, savory and sweet, and an assortment of fruits, and then she removed that smooth gold ring her finger was never without and tied it to a leaf of one of the rice plants. When all of that was done, she sat down on the ground with her legs folded to one side and prayed for a long time. That was the year that, after the ceremony, we had to double back— she'd forgotten her ring. I am a child of the jungle, and yet so, so much of it is an enigma to me. Peacocks, for example—an absolute enigma to me. Peacocks are a noble and truly exquisite bird, and they possess a beautiful song—one used to hear it ringing like a bell, out to the edges of the forest. Peacocks are truly the gems of the jungle, the most glamorous stars of the forest's grand drama. I like to indulge in the fantasy that peacocks are creatures of the Himmapan Forest, and not of the forests of this earth. In my fantasy, they feed on ether and on pure dewdrops and not on grasshoppers. It's a complete mystery to me why heavenly birds like peacocks should have to come and romance one another in the world beneath. Male peacocks are more striking than peahens, and will strut up and down the forest glade, with their tails outspread, to flaunt themselves to the females. It's truly a divine performance. But before they fan their feathers and begin their mating dance, the cocks first trim down and neaten up the glade; they twirl their graceful necks around tall blades of grass and yank them out, and twirl again and yank more out, inspecting the readiness of their stage the same way an expert dancer would do before a performance, and hunters used to kill them by furtively planting in the glade the need to go and eat crabs. Monkeys are peculiar creatures. When it's pouring out, they'll sit up in trees, shivering in misery. And if the rain won't let up, they'll break off branches and twigs and lay them across different boughs and spread leaves over them, creating something that looks like a pretty sturdy, well-sealed roof. If they were to go down and hide under that roof, they'd at least be protected from the rain. Monkeys do build houses, which is what those things are. But once they're satisfied with the construction, for some absurd reason, they'll go and sit on top of the roof and keep shivering there. It confounds me why, after going through the trouble of assembling themselves shelter, they'd let themselves continue to be tormented by the rain. One year, a troop of monkeys came and raided Mae Duangbulan's cornfields, causing extensive damage. Old Man Junpa was livid when he heard and hatched a plan. He boiled up some moonshine, that being something he'd had plenty of practice doing anyway, and placed numerous jars of it out in the cornfields, in the parts that had mostly been spared from damage. Then he chopped river-tamarind wood into sticks, each as fat as a wrist and about an arm's length, and left a bundle of them out near the jars of moonshine. And then the monkeys showed up. Leading the way were the troop's commander and four or five of his lieutenants. The rest of the troop hung back, waiting for their signal. The alpha and his henchmen all started imbibing, and soon got into a festive mood, feeling euphoric from the effect of the giggle juice. They signaled for the rest of the gang to come and join them, and at first, they shared the moonshine, taking turns to drink, and the spirit was communal, and all was cordial and amicable. After a while, though, the monkeys got drunk and started fighting. Probably one of them had said something that had rubbed one of the other ones the wrong way, and they started to bite, shove, limes. If you have a daughter in her prime, I'll trade you a son-in-law," where do you think those lyrics came from? There'd be a lot of haggling back and forth before people would settle on an exchange. Nobody tried to take advantage of anybody. Even sellers from distant tambons like Poriang, Poloy, Waang Takhian, or Huay Sua or Nern Sakae would make the effort to row over here to hawk their wares. By the pier out in front of the temple up to a hundred boats, big and small, would be gathered. It was always a scene of great hubbub and hullabaloo. I'll probably never have the chance to see a market like that again in this life. Every time the Kathin Festival was on at Praeknamdang Temple, too, boats big and small would gather by the pier out in front of the temple. The festival sponsors would have meals ready to hand out to attendants: there'd be white rice, chili dip of unripe tamarind, fried mackerel and raw vegetables, all wrapped in lotus leaf, plus two or three tangerines. After a long row to make it over, you really savored a meal like that. I always needed seconds to satisfy my appetite. I'll probably never have the chance to see a Kathin Festival like that again in this life and will probably never have the chance to encounter people like that again, such fine, sunny, good-natured people, jungle folk who were genuine and candid, good to each other openly, bad to each other openly. Thieves in those days, before they'd rob somebody's house, would first plant a sign to alert the homeowners. The landscape didn't look so exposed and empty the way it does now. People occupied and cleared land in small patches only, just enough to make room for a house and to grow rice and a few other crops. The jungle was still dense and thick back then. Tigers still roamed around in these parts. The jungle was still deeply enchanted. The mysterious forces of the jungle and its spirits and ghosts were still sacred. But then forest concessions stripped the jungle bare. And

and yellow like moonlight. In the jungle, even in the full light of day, even when I was trekking with Old Man Junpa or with other grown-ups, a tiger's growl, however far away it was, made my heart skip a beat. And during those times when I was less than well-behaved and wandered off playing, as children do, a tiger's growl, even from afar, even in the full light of day, triggered a rash of goosebumps all over my body. When a tiger revealed itself, no matter where, all the different animals would call out frenzied, panicked warnings to their own kind, and next thing you knew, silence would spread through that part of the jungle. But sometimes, the jungle was quiet all on its own, and I could never quite tell whether the jungle was simply quiet on its own or whether a tiger was on the scene. But after a tiger's growl was heard, the jungle would fall even more hushed and remain hushed for a long time. Different birds and monkeys and lemurs and such and even squirrels and their cousins would fall silent and hold still. All the animals of the jungle would lie low, waiting until they were certain the tiger had passed through before they would stir again, or make the slightest sound. While in the jungle, whether I was accompanied by Old Man Junpa or somebody else, if I heard a tiger, I'd immediately look around, scanning for an escape route or for a place to hide. But the jungle always seemed poor in hiding places and escape routes. Jump in the water? Tigers can swim. Climb up a tree? Tigers can do the same. Stand or walk, sit or duck down on the ground, run for your life or stay stock-still—none of it ever seemed like a wise course of action, and all I ever did was sit or stand where I was when I'd heard the tiger's growl, watching my front, my sides, my back, feeling as though that intensely green world, thick and opaque with flora, contained nothing but me and the tiger. The truly horrific part was, be it day or night, I always felt dense with large, imposing trees; their branches arched and met in the middle, forming a seamless canopy threaded together with an assortment of vines, turning the passage underneath into something like a tunnel. On the ground, an underbrush of weeds and grass grew on top of each other. Back then I never worked hard when less would do, and soon enough I let the water carry the boat at its own lackadaisical pace as I lay prone, chin hooked on the gunwale, peering through the limpid depth of the stream—haste was the last thing on my mind. The world beneath the water was soundless, peaceful, and cool to the eye; it was full of grass, seaweed, duck lettuce, and lotus clusters, full of shrimp, mollusks, crabs, and fish. I gazed at the river snails latched to the stems of reeds, at the striped snakeheads suspended among the duck lettuce, still but for the fins fluttering by their ears and the tails wavering just at the tips. I gazed at the crabs scuttling clumsily on the muddy bank. I gazed at the hydrillas swaying in the soft current like tree branches blowing in the wind. All of it was novel and sublime, strange and beautiful, tranquil and intriguing, and refreshing to look at, and I lay in enraptured reverie, as I always did on this journey. One giant mudfish, a new mother, patiently took up the rear behind her children—there must have been a hundred of them, tinier than matchsticks—and with my boat approaching, she gaped her mouth open for all of her offspring to take shelter within as I watched, wonder-struck. A school of red-tailed tinfoil barbs swam wiggling back and forth around a patch of blue lotus flowers; with their bright silver scales dazzling, they looked as though they weren't living things but rather jewels fit for a splendid heroine. Now hampala barbs shot through the water like pewter fireworks. With all this wonder beneath and around me, I didn't notice the strange silence that had fallen over the world above at all. Under a cluster the people of Praeknamdang was that the tiger had claimed two lives in that incident: Mae Duangbulan's and her son Kwantien's. But I survived, I reemerged into reality. However, I couldn't break free of that sheer, indescribable terror. It would take me ten years to conquer it, and the victory came at a steep price, perhaps too steep. In response to Mae Duangbulan's end, Old Man Junpa became a mighty tiger slayer. Two days after her death, instead of staying and looking after me, his ailing son, he left me in Luang Paw Kom's care and returned to that same fig tree, where he captured the murderous tiger. He showed no attachment toward Mae Duangbulan's body and used none other than her corpse to bait the tiger. That was how much he wanted revenge. And how heartless and barbaric he could be. He didn't kill the tiger with a single shot. His Ninlagaan tame in his hands, he shattered its legs one by one, bullet by bullet, calmly, intending to kill it slowly, bent on a cold revenge. The tiger thrashed on the ground, growling ferociously as it sent grass whipping in every direction. Old Man Junpa shot it twice more, in the flank and in the spine, methodical enough not to kill it and mindful enough not to leave it able to attack him. He cut down a vine, looped it around the tiger's neck, and dragged the creature out of the forest, all the way to the clearing in the middle of the village, mouthing curse words the whole way. In the clearing (or so went the story going around Praeknamdang at the time, which matched the account later shared with me directly), he hammered down two posts and tied the tiger's two forelegs and two hind legs tight to each of the posts. He ran a flame along its skin, he pricked it with thorns, kicked it with the front of his foot, with the back of his heel, spat on it, pissed on it. He'd gone mad, and he looked it, his hair wild, his eyes raging and bloodshot, his whole body quivering with tension and cruelty. For days, he never wandered far from the trap strung to a tree, its sole aim being to kill tigers. He built cage traps tirelessly, and time and time again he left the unlucky tiger to rot right in the contraption without ever dismantling it. He once snatched tiger cubs from their lair after waiting for their mother to go out in search of food, and noosed their necks with vines and hung them in a row over the mouth of their den. He went out and bought me a percussion rifle of my own, which he named Sai Fah Faad—Thunderbolt—and by training me himself, made a sharp, agile shooter out of me (when I was new to it, Sai Fah Faad kicked me over and over, nearly knocking my shoulder out of joint). He had me accompany him into the jungle, teaching me how to follow tiger trails and hunt like a grown man. But when the moment came to shoot a tiger, I could never muster the courage to do it. Every time I was about to pull the trigger, my mind couldn't help but flash back to the shock and horror, the pain and suffering, that Mae Duangbulan had had to endure. Deep down, I always thought I'd be dealt the same fate as Mae Duangbulan, and instead of driving me on, the thought paralyzed me. Every time I had to shoot a tiger, when the moment of truth came, Old Man Junpa had to step in and do it. He grew beyond exasperated with me, and, using the harshest, crudest words, would chastise and belittle me, right there over the body of the tiger he had just shot on my behalf. For the most part, Old Man Junpa's strategy was to trail a tiger and shoot it in the daytime, but sometimes his tactic was to sit in wait up on a machan at night, near to where he'd found a tiger's prey, particularly when the moon shone bright enough, because tigers tend not to polish off their prey in one go; instead, they usually retrace their steps and come back to eat the rest later. I'd help him set up the machan, camouflaging it with greenery, and then we'd get ourselves up there and sit from the first hints of evening, and keep on sitting in the same position, however stiff we got. Every time you wanted to shift any part of your body, you had to do it as quietly and carefully as possible. Horseflies and mosquitoes and midges and mites would crawl or land on us and suck our blood until they were full and swollen. You couldn't risk making a noise by hitting or slapping them and had to try and brush them off gently with your hand. If you needed to piss, you had to piss into a bamboo tube. If you needed to shit, tough luck, you had to hold it. And you couldn't come down from the machan until day broke, and as far as I could see, the machan was always perilously close to the carcass—only about three or four arm spans away sometimes—and to me, the machan we were on never seemed high enough, it always seemed a tiger could leap right up onto it in one go, and boy, the sickening odor of the prey! In the moonlight, so full of illusions, and amid the silence, after a long, excruciating wait, I'd eventually hear a tiger approaching, returning to its meal. Tigers haunt the day too, but of course their might burns brightest at night, and in that moonlight so full of illusions, I'd spot a pair of petrifying, scintillating emerald eyes among the trees, eyes that had the ability to stun and mesmerize me as if they could actually hypnotize. They were eyes more powerful than any other animal's, far more powerful than humans'. Those eyes seemed to say to me: "Come, come close. Come and have a good look at me. I'm a thing of wonder. Or would you rather I go up there to you?" and then in me would arise the desire to climb down to the owner of those eyes, or else have the owner of those eyes come up to me. It was that way every time I saw a tiger's eyes at night. I was spellbound; it was as though I were sleepwalking, unable to distinguish between illusion and reality, fixed in a mesmerized state as though I were hypnotized, my mind thinking of nothing but Mae Duangbulan, thinking about nothing but what her reactions would have been, what her thoughts, been with me that evening, who can say what might have happened? I could be a dead man. I'm getting goosebumps just from telling the story. Here, look at my arms! I'm getting tingles down the front of my neck, too, thinking how close I came to having those fangs in my throat. That cursed tiger, struck by Old Man Junpa's ten-saleung lead bullet, was sent writhing on the ground below a big makha tree. The creature was stunned, it was furious, it was in horrific pain. It attempted to get back on its feet, it eyed Old Man Junpa, it eyed me, and made as if it was about to spring at Old Man Junpa, but then it staggered and keeled over once more, letting loose an earthshaking roar. Then all of a sudden, it lost interest in Old Man Junpa, who was hurrying to repack his rifle with gunpowder and a new bullet, lost interest in me, who the whole time had been standing there stunned, with a dead muntjac draped over my shoulders, wet and sticky with blood from the carcass, awkwardly frozen like a coward—it lost interest in us completely. It thrashed about, now rolling onto its stomach, now rolling onto its back, and it groaned and growled in agony, its body contracting and expanding, its long tail flailing and out of control—and *that* made it livid. It curled its tail toward itself, its body arced, and it bit down on its own tail and chewed without mercy two or three times. But then it realized, no, its tail wasn't to blame for its host of impairments, it was rather its right foreleg, which now hung stiffly, it was rather this limb that was the culprit, this limb that failed to respond, that no longer obeyed its command, and so it rolled over and laid its belly flat against the ground, opened its jaws and bared its fangs all the way, and bit down on its right foreleg as hard as it could, above the paw, which caused its paw to be severed off, its paw which it then cast aside without any sentimentality, and it bit down once again just as hard on that same leg, higher than before, sinking its cattle jabbed with such a prod tastes wrong. Old Man Junpa would often grow exasperated with me and say, "Why are you going to let tigers make you shake in your shoes? All they are is a kind of cat," and he was convinced of it too. He liked to leave me with a tiger's carcass for long stretches at a time. I'd try to get used to the dead tiger, try to overcome my fear, and every time I was about to have to get in there and skin a tiger, although I'd start by standing some distance away and hesitating and staring at the dead tiger from that distance and taking much too long to work up the nerve, eventually I'd approach and squat down next to it and, after hesitating for a long while more, pry its maw open, study its fangs and teeth, study them with care, study even its red and incredibly rough tongue, study its claws, those big, sharp, hornlike claws, those claws concealed within its paws and once ever ready to unfurl—I'd study and touch and feel them; and I'd pull apart its eyelids to study its eyes, which had the color of yellow sapphires in the daytime and which morphed into the deep green of emeralds at night; I'd run my hand along its fur, reversing from its hind to its head, and study in detail the yellow portions and the black portions along its spine and flanks, and the white areas under its belly, under its chin, under its neck, all of which sometimes had fleas buried within, and study and touch its skin (it's a thin-skinned animal), study its long, curved tail, which consisted of a column of bones stacked from large to small, and study its nipples, which both male and female tigers have, and lift up the tail to study its behind, study its rear hole, lift up its leg and hold that high to study its pathetic penis and testicles (or, in the case of a tigress, study its yoni), and I'd skin it and carve open its belly to study its intestines, its stomach, its liver, its lungs, its heart (I've been tempted to eat a tiger's heart before, eat it raw, eat it so I'd never again fear another tiger in this world), ears, and belted out its own *baroooh!* before charging straight at the locomotive. The driver didn't ease up, and when the two met, the poor elephant was struck and killed on the spot, right over the track. The locomotive skidded off the rails and ended up as a pile of rusting junk in the grass. But unlike the elephant, the driver survived—which is hardly fair, I say. That bastard! How dare he crash into an elephant and kill it like that. The idiot should have known to slow down; he was a guest on the elephant's land. Old Man Junpa always drilled it into me that I must never kill an elephant under any circumstances; rather, I was to be patient with them and forgiving toward them and treat them like my own older brothers and sisters. At the same time, though, he didn't hesitate to show me the clean-kill spots for boars and muntjacs and deer and gaurs and tigers, and as time passed and I began to grow up, I became a respectably sharp shooter, and I started to be able to withstand the gun's kicks, and I grew adept enough at navigating the jungle that I never, ever got lost—the jungle in these parts, in particular, I knew like the back of my hand—and I was well-trained enough to be able to take my rifle and venture into the jungle alone at night, and in certain respects I think I developed into a more prudent and watchful hunter than Old Man Junpa was. I was no lightweight as a huntsman, and I might have been regarded as a truly grand hunter had I just possessed enough courage to shoot even a single tiger. I told you just now I wasn't afraid to head into the jungle alone at night, and that was true, but only if I was sure that it was a part of the jungle which was, at that time, free of tigers. At night, the jungle was replete with mysterious sounds, mysterious silences, mysterious darknesses, and mysterious shadows. If any of you find yourself alone in the jungle at night with those sounds, those silences, those darknesses, and those shadows, and you attempt climbing up to the top to smoke bees, where there were numerous beehives, large and small, maybe even a hundred of them. At that hour, the morning fog still had the forest engulfed in its white haze, and dew clung to blades of grass in fat, glistening drops, and wild chickens were still crowing and flapping their wings in loud *flups*, and the perfume of dwarf ylang-ylangs hung in the air. Then from up high I spotted, out of nowhere, a tiger running at full gallop, hot on the heels of a boar. They zigzagged this way and that way, now going to the left, now going to the right. The boar, because it was still unharmed, wasn't going to risk a fight, even though it had a fearsome pair of tusks at its disposal. Instead, it squealed like a common pig and cannonballed into the swamp. The tiger followed it into the water, and the boar kicked and hoofed, trying to swim away. Both of them, though land animals, are good swimmers, and although the boar kept fleeing farther and farther away from the shore, the tiger kept relentlessly on its tail. Soon, it was near enough to pounce, and it launched itself at the boar, biting it in the hind leg before it spun around, ready to paddle back with its prey gripped between its teeth. But then it was forced to stop in its tracks: in front of it, a large, long crocodile was floating silently in the water, and, without prelude, the crocodile clamped its jaw onto the boar's neck. The poor boar ran from a tiger right into a crocodile, quite literally, like in the saying. Crocodiles' jaws are a hideous sight to behold: jagged and craggy, ancient and mighty, lined with yellow, irregular fangs and teeth. The crocodile openly wanted the boar for itself, and with its superior strength and terrain advantage, it was able to tow it, along with the tiger, which still refused to let go of the boar's hind leg, into deep water. The tiger did attempt to drag the boar back in its direction, but its strength was outmatched by the crocodile's, and both boar and tiger were idle curiosity, and it had probably long gone off to find itself some fish elsewhere. Regardless, it had made the tiger paranoid. The tiger was still waiting when the sun dropped below the treetops and gibbons were starting up their evening whines and a large cloud of bats emerged, sluggish-winged, out looking for food. (These bats had claimed a grove of wild mangoes as their sleeping place, and the leaves on every single one of the trees there were brown and shriveled because of the effect of their shit and piss, coats and coats of which had accumulated.) The tiger had bided its time, by that point having waited for a full ten hours. Only then, when it trusted that the situation was truly safe, did it venture into the water, seize the boar's carcass and haul it in. Can you believe its determination? And the implacability of its predatory instinct? But there, you see? Even tigers are scared of crocodiles. Strangely, though, I'm not scared of crocodiles at all. Back in those days, during the high-water season, when russet water would wash over and flood the lowlands, many, many parts were transformed into great big swamps. In places, they were so deep you couldn't reach the bottom with an entire length of a spiny bamboo. It was in these swamps that I used to hunt crocodiles. I'd take a long bamboo pole that had been sharpened to a point and plunge it hard into the water, and while holding onto the pole, I'd stir the water with my feet. A crocodile would soon swim over, and I'd float with my body prone and parallel to the surface, making sure to face the crocodile head-on. It couldn't then charge and bite me because the bamboo pole would be in the way. Wherever it maneuvered itself for the attack, I'd always maneuver myself to be directly opposite from it. Crocodiles don't know to dive down and get at their prey from underneath. All they know how to do is swim like a stiff log straight at their prey and nip them at surface level. And when they don't get their way, they become even more ferocious and yawn their jaws wide. At that point, I'd toss over a piece of tiger's claw wood, one about the size of a calf, that I would have brought with me, to give its eager jaws something to bite down on. Tiger's claw is a soft wood, and when the crocodile's teeth sank into the flesh of the wood, its mouth would be stuck shut. Now it was toothless, and no better than a floating log. I'd then loop it with a sisal rope and tie it up, and Old Man Junpa would row over and tether it side by side to the boat. The following day, Old Man Junpa would pole the boat into town and sell the crocodile. I've caught crocodile after crocodile using this method—large crocodiles, too, a ton of them. Like I said, I was a child of the jungle, and I became a man in the jungle. I've committed myriad sins in my life. I've taken myriad lives of myriad animals . . . Most people of that time, no matter where in the country they lived, used this method of catching crocodiles, but there were those who had a specific antipathy toward them and were far crueler. These people would go out with short sections of monastery bamboo, about a handspan or two long, sharpened to a keen point at both ends. When a crocodile parted its maw for them to see, they'd ram one of these bamboo sticks into the bottom of its mouth and promptly withdraw their hand. In pain and anger, the crocodile would bite down with its full force, which meant the sharpened ends of the bamboo would pierce through both the roof and floor of its mouth, resulting in a slow and painful and agonizing death. But this is something I've never seen with my own eyes, I've only heard of it secondhand. I believe the stories are true, though, because people are cruel and crocodiles are stupid. It's all too easy to take advantage of their habit of snapping at things. What I *have* seen with my own eyes is crocodile hunting using redbird cacti: what you do is cut a big armful of redbird cacti, pound them to get hammer in another one a step higher and to the left, and step onto that one with your left foot, and you'd keep going and going like that until you reached the top. Once you'd finished your business with the bees, you climbed back down, pulling the stakes out one by one and dropping them back in your bag. Once again, it was Old Man Junpa who passed on this skill to me, and I was a natural at it. I'm not afraid of heights, you see. Year-round, both Old Man Junpa and I could eat honey to our hearts' content, and we always had enough left to barter with at the flea market; we even had enough to be able to put some aside and sell in town. Collecting honey like that, which required you to be up in a treetop, led to my witnessing strange things that I would wager no one else has ever seen. One evening, while I was perched high in a rubber tree, about to start a fire for bee smoking, I heard low, soft grunts from below: *oin, oin, oin.* It sounded like a boar, even a warmhearted mother boar, whose call her piglets would be well familiar with, perhaps a caring mother boar who'd stumbled upon taros or potatoes or some other roots or maybe an ample patch of wild sweet greens, but when my eyes found where the sound was coming from, I saw that, hiding in the bushes beneath me, it was in fact a tiger! I was high above, peering down, and my eyes weren't playing tricks on me. But I couldn't believe my ears, I didn't understand why on earth a tiger was mimicking the call of a mother boar—that is, until I heard four piglets. They were wallowing in a puddle of mud not far from where the tiger was crouched down hiding and grunting like a pig. They couldn't have been long weaned; the melon pattern on their fur was still distinct. The largest of the piglets, which was the greediest one too, heard the oinking and immediately made straight to the source of the sound. It walked itself straight into the tiger's mouth, really. The tiger gobbled it up, then licked its lips and licked its paws for a long while before ambling off. The other three piglets, I'm pleased to say, managed to escape. But tigers *are* more cunning and more dangerous than Old Man Junpa supposed them to be. Once, while up in a tree on another occasion of bee smoking, I even got to witness monkeys—low, graceless animals, fidgety and unrestrained in manner—laughing at a tiger, as if they were superior! There was a tribe of monkeys up in the crown of a black plum tree, and at first when they spotted a tiger approaching down below, they trailed off with that ugly *eek, ook-ook* sound they make. The tiger was a scrawny one, so scrawny its waist was sunken and the skin under its belly was loose and flapping from side to side. It was old, and undignified in appearance, with patches of fur missing and a painful-looking wound on its hind leg—it might have been gored by a boar or a deer—and it was lumbering along very slowly. It glanced up at the monkeys in the plum tree, who cried out for the others in their cohort to be on guard: *Look out, elders among us! Look out, little ones! A villain's on the prowl down there,* or so they seemed to be saying. Then they managed silence for several whole breaths, but soon, being that they don't know how to keep still, they began to swing themselves from branch to branch, and then they stopped and bared their teeth, looking down. Upon finding themselves safe, they began to screech and rock the plum branches, getting more and more rowdy and excited. The monkeys seemed to taunt and mock the tiger, saying something like: *If you're so big and scary, why don't you come up here? What's wrong? Cat got your tongue?* The tiger didn't react. It trailed around, without much energy. Then it disappeared into the dense bushes full of thorns below the black plum tree, hiding with its entire body, except for its long, bowed tail curling at the tip. It stayed hidden for a long time. At first, I figured it was going to try imitating the call of a mother quills. In return, she gave me sweets like foytong, tongyip, tongyawd, and galamare. I brought her bamboo shoots and termite mushrooms and wild sweet greens and venison. In return, she gave me sticky rice and sesame seeds and coconuts and beans and sugar. I brought her punk wood to use as tinder, and she gave me a khao mah cloth for me to wear around my waist. Our love, from the start, was such plain sailing. After I announced to Old Man Junpa my intention to take a wife, he arranged to go ask for her hand for me, giving over as her bridewealth a gold necklace weighing one baht. Then I picked up Garagade in my boat and brought her home to live with me in Praeknamdang. Right away, Garagade started planting rice—in unirrigated fields, which were all we had—and started planting gourds and cucumbers and such, and chilis and beans, and she put a lot of effort into finding flowering and other decorative plants to grow in our garden. As for me and Old Man Junpa, we still made regular trips into the jungle, to hunt and to gather things we could sell. Each time Old Man Junpa and I were about to leave, Garagade's face would turn long, because our departure meant she'd be left all by herself for days at a time. She was also worried about me, fearing danger would come my way in the jungle. As a young woman, being home alone must have been intimidating for her, and Praeknamdang in those days was only a small enclave in the middle of the wilderness, the whole village being made up of twelve dwellings, unlike Po-Ain, which until then had been the only home she'd known. Po-Ain was a sizable village, surrounded by open skies and wide paddy fields. They had copses of toddy palms, their crowns making peaks and troughs on the horizon, and had patches of brushwood; in fact, it looked pretty much like Praeknamdang does today. The people over there mainly farmed. They took growing rice seriously, took tilling land seriously, and their fields were subdivided into plots, which they framed with bunds as they saw fit. They didn't just dig a little hole and drop seeds in and step on it like you did with rice grown in level fields. Garagade was frustrated when she found herself having to work with unirrigated fields like that. Farming rice in Praeknamdang, you didn't get to reap all of what you sowed, no, not like with proper, wet-paddy-grown rice. What's more, she wasn't accustomed to having to barter for rice. For her entire life, she'd always been able to count on her family's barn having more rice than they could eat, and that was true year-round, and it wasn't long before she began to express her desire to find a suitable plot of land for farming rice properly. From then on, whenever she realized I was about to head into the jungle again, she refused to stay home and watch the house. Instead, she implored me to row her back to Po-Ain to visit her parents. Arguing wasn't her way; she preferred to protest in silence. She wanted me to stop hunting and properly take up rice farming; she thought this would provide greater stability and give the two of us the chance to live a normal, happy life as husband and wife. The parcel of land that Old Man Junpa had taken over for Mae Duangbulan to grow rice and other crops, bordering the stream and located south of the village, consisted of only five rais. Old Man Junpa told Garagade he'd give it to her outright, and she could decide if she wanted to dig into the ground and raise levees to farm rice. Garagade, however, said five rais wouldn't suffice, she wanted at least thirty or forty. So, on the ninth day of the waning moon in the third month of 2437 BE, I found myself leading my wife through the forest, making a full day's journey eastward on foot, because I had a place in mind, one that was to my heart's liking. In fact, it was Mae Duangbulan who'd shown me the spot, back when I was seven or eight years old. The tract was a clearing in the jungle, a large, still fixed in the soil. We decided we'd wait until the following year to turn the rest of the land, which was another fifteen rais or so, into paddy fields. The soil was dark and loamy. Garagade planted pumpkins streamside, and in no time they pushed out verdurous vines and sunny yellow blossoms and rough, bumpy fruit the size of rice buckets. She deposited some ridge gourd seeds streamside, and in no time the gourds started growing and growing, yielding fruit as big as thighs. She planted wing bean seeds too, and in no time the beans started climbing up the garden stakes, their flowers and pods quickly proliferating. Her bird's eye chilis and spur chilies also thrived and soon bore white flowers and pepper pods, and the ginger, galangal, and lemongrass all showed up as if conjured, and grew and flourished. The time Garagade spent planting vegetables, I spent making a beam for our plow, and Old Man Junpa spent making a harrow. The time she spent out with a shovel neatening up the bunds in the paddies, I spent cutting down bamboo trees to build a shed for the oxen, and Old Man Junpa spent cutting down bamboo trees to build a rice barn. The time Garagade spent collecting wild mangoes—they littered the forest floor, and she made candied mango mash with them—I spent that time foraging for young bamboo shoots, and Old Man Junpa spent it toting his rifle through the jungle to shoot muntjacs and other deer. My cattle shed was soon completed. The posts and rails were bamboo, the thatch was cogon grass, the frame of the roof was bamboo and solid, and I even fitted it with mangers. The whole structure was compact and sturdy, lying a little west of the hut. On the other side of the hut, to the east, Old Man Junpa's rice barn was soon ready too. The columns were hardwood, the walls and the floor, which was elevated from the ground, were clay-coated bamboo, the thatch was cogon grass, the frame of the roof was bamboo and solid and

strong, and he had even fitted it with front steps. We all vied to do
the most work, bragging about our own achievements and scoffing
at each other's, all in good fun. We ate heartily, turned in late and
rose before the sun—there was always much to be accomplished.
We worked as a united team, but at the same time, it was a sport for
us to compete. Old Man Junpa was the instigator of this game. He
didn't want to simply put his head down and work, and instead did
his best to find the fun in all our endeavors. And bright and early one
morning at the start of summer that year, the three of us set out on a
journey through the jungle, passing back through Praeknamdang
and continuing on to Po-Ain. In Po-Ain, Garagade removed the one-
baht gold necklace that had been given to her as her bridewealth and
handed it over to a fellow named Chote, who owned a large herd of
cattle, and she chose for us four young oxen that had never been put
to work, all of them already castrated, all of them already nose-roped.
And then, riding our new oxen part of the way and leading them part
of the way, we traversed the thickness of the jungle back to our hut. It
didn't take long before Garagade gave them names: Din, Naam,
Lom, and Fai—Earth, Water, Air, and Fire. She also came up with
the name for the land we'd made home: Nern Tago Dum—Ebony
Knoll. That year, the rain arrived early, at the start of the sixth month,
and the water came down as though the sky were full of holes.
Garagade and I set about ploughing and harrowing. With virgin
forest land like that, you had to plow it over at least twice and harrow
it over at least twice again. And our oxen, having never worked
before, hemmed and hawed every step of the way, we made ourselves
hoarse yelling at them. And it wasn't as if I knew my way around a
plow or a harrow. Garagade kept having to teach me, to show me
how. Old Man Junpa came and hovered or hung around nearby,
watching, at times booing at me or shaking his head. The fun of it

began to emerge from the soil, field crabs and apple snails from who knows where showed up and helped themselves to our crop. She kept killing off these pests, and when *they* were finally gotten rid of, a flock of little parrots, green with reddish beaks, came down and, too, ate what they liked. So she made a scarecrow, and under its guard the nursery turned emerald and lush and luxuriant. She always knew exactly what to do. She knew when the nursery plot needed to be drained, and when it needed to be flooded. When she saw that the seedlings were almost a cubit tall, she pulled them out of the soil and ferried them over to another plot that was already well tilled, and then she went about resetting them into the ground, the distance between each bunch perfectly uniform, the rows straight and perfectly parallel. I'd never farmed that way before, working with seedlings and flooded fields. Garagade constantly had to direct me, constantly keep after me. She was the leader and I the follower. She knew all kinds of things that I had no idea about. Next to her, I was such an amateur, and watching her, I couldn't help but marvel. The newly transplanted seedlings were at first sickly yellow, and their leaves were brown and shriveled at the tips, but after a while, they gained their footing and turned a vivid green, and then they grew and grew. What a contrast it was from growing rice unirrigated, and I couldn't help but marvel at it all. When we plowed and harrowed the fields, Garagade used Din and Naam, harnessed side by side, while I used Lom and Fai, harnessed side by side. She led the way and I followed, and when hard at work, she was as tough and tenacious as any man, certainly as I, and Mae Posop, she was gracious to us, she was never fussy, she grew like a dream, she sprang lavish leaves in prominent bunches, she soon tillered, she rose in voluptuous stalks. At the conclusion of each day's work, I couldn't help but take a minute to marvel: the miracle fish flapping at the tips of the tines. In certain moments, Old Man Junpa, with a trident in hand, resembled a sea god; at other times, though, he could have been a demonic Asura right out of an ancient epic. When night fell, he headed out with a torch to catch frogs. Sinning became the man. During that period, he was happy, often tipsy, always in a fine mood; you could catch him crooning likay tunes in his own wonky way. After each day's work in the fields, I'd lead the oxen into the stream and bathe them one by one, scrubbing them until they were immaculate. The oxen loved to be bathed—they couldn't wait to get the mud off them. Once done, I'd steer them back to their shed, and Garagade would fetch them wild bananas and sprigs of river tamarind, and she'd sickle grass for them and pile it in tall baskets for them to eat. Our oxen may have been worn out and battered from being worked from sunup to sundown, but they were well fed and nicely bathed, and they slept in a clean, sturdy shed. All four of them were playful; they were still young and so were still rambunctious and curious like children. After their baths, they'd get rowdy and chase each other around and butt heads, all in good fun—they were merely testing out their own strength. Sometimes they'd come over to me and try to get *me* to fight them—they'd use their horns to nudge me, sometimes in the back, sometimes in the shoulder, and then they'd back away, swing their hinds to one side, drop their heads low and glare at me, and all of sudden, they'd snort and drop the whole act and walk over to me, looking like they were about to dissolve into laughter, act apologetic, and insist on licking my face, my ears, my head. Sometimes they'd go over to Garagade and try to get *her* to fight them—they'd use their horns to nudge her, sometimes in the back, sometimes in the shoulder, and Garagade would laugh—her laughter was so bright and cheerful—and she would scold them and pet them on the playful as a young girl. When she had time, she would head into the forest with a shovel to find fragrant varieties of plants to dig up and bring home, and the way she planted them in our hut's front yard— in long lines and nicely distanced—you'd think she had ambitions for a botanical garden of her own. And she continued to climb trees to pick ripe fruit, and to check bird's nests for laid eggs. There was a serene, contented smile on her lips, and in her eyes, and her beauty and her liveliness grew quietly, like a flower in the rainy season. Along the stream, the torch gingers produced an extravagant number of blossoms in white and in magenta, each one of them staying pert and open for a month before wilting and dropping off. Lotuses, red or ultramarine, spread their scent far and wide, luring giant honeybees to come and loll inside them and inhale their perfume. Bread-flower plants budded and rambled high, high up along tall trees, flowering white against the bark; and jumpoons bloomed and shed their blossoms below, and the air was infused with the sweet fragrance of all of these flowers, and that sweetness had a depth and richness you just don't smell now. The sarapi tree outside our hut adorned itself with innumerable white flowers, which later dropped and dotted the hut's and the barn's and the cattle shed's roofs, the rest carpeting the ground. Cicadas trilled, and crickets and their cousins chirped, and swarms of bees buzzed as they flew about ever in search of nectar, and everywhere flitted kaleidoscopes of butterflies. Only one thing was irksome, which was that all of our hens and our rooster had been snatched away and eaten by palm civets . . . But that was just part of living out there in the jungle. Some nights, after the rain ceased or as it lightened to a drizzle, the entire forest turned sapphire blue, gleaming and glistering from the tens or hundreds of thousands of fireflies that made it appear festooned for a festival. The lights of innumerable fireflies like that is something I'll probably never have the chance to see again in this life. Those lights and the way they shimmered and twinkled rendered the jungle more splendid than paradise. Every evening gibbons whined, loud and plaintive, as the sky warmed to the color of ripe betel nuts. There were nights, when the moon shone bright, I heard peacocks squawking from boughs high in a tree. It's a mystery how the moon, so old and ancient, appears ever radiant and fair. Some nights, if she wasn't too exhausted, Garagade would play her saw for me, its sound taking on a melancholic note in the quiet, and she would sing her timeworn tunes, which were slow and dulcet, songs that weren't anything but testaments to the gaiety of a girlhood full of hopes, full of dreams, and yet unmarred by any of life's darkness or bitterness, and I'd lounge next to her on the bamboo daybed in front of the hut, thinking how beautiful the sound of her fiddle and of her song were. Some nights, by the lamplight, she would read *Siriwibulkit* or *Khun Chang Khun Phaen* to me. Her books couldn't have been shabbier or more dog-eared, their covers in tatters; these were books, after all, that had been printed when Dr. Bradley and Reverend Smith still ran their printing houses. But there were other nights, too, when she neither played me music nor read to me, and those were nights when the cicadas were a big mahori symphony of their own, stridulating endlessly into the dark hours, and both she and I would simply sit or lie quietly, listening to them, and I'd feel as though I didn't have a care in the world, and I'd let myself dream again and again of the time our rice would sprout ears, of the time our harvest would arrive, and I'd let myself dream ahead, too, of clearing more of the forest land and expanding our paddy fields farther and farther out. As for my four oxen, I was already planning that, once the year's tilling was complete, I'd give them taguay to make them pass worms, and I'd indulge them and fatten them up, tucking seedlings into the soil. Early morning on another day, a young stag wandered out of the forest and stood there, wide-eyed and awestruck, watching Garagade and me as we plowed, and then, curious, approached closer, eventually staying in the nearby scrub and nibbling vines as if we were no danger at all. But alas, in the quiet hours nearing dawn on the tenth night of the waxing moon in the seventh month of that year, in the middle of the darkness and silence and in the warm damp of the misting rain, Old Man Junpa, Garagade and I were startled awake, all of us at once. In the cattle shed beside the hut, the oxen wailed and scrambled in chaos, yanking on their lead ropes, rattling hard the bamboo rails they were tied to. Then came the sound of the shed's fence collapsing, along with shrieks of pain and panic coming from one of the oxen. I lit a torch, threw open the hut's door and rushed out. In the cattle shed, standing amid the thin white smoke still lingering from the fire, I counted only three oxen, all of them trembling, all of them straining on their ropes, all of them with their heads dropped and eyes bulging, all of them tensely shivering, horror-stricken and terrified, the legs on all of them limp as though about to give—and that's how oxen look a few breaths out from an encounter with a tiger! Din was nowhere to be seen. On the damp ground inside the shed, there appeared not only hoofprints but also paw prints and blood, which had splattered onto the fence too. One set of the hoof marks was only the cloven toes of an ox scratching along the earth, making plain the tiger had sunk its teeth into the ox's scruff and dragged it away. The tiger's paw prints also made plain it was lame and hobbled with its left forepaw not landing firmly on the ground, but also that it was a big, strong tiger. The fence reached up to my chest, but the beast was large enough to have snatched Din and leapt up onto it with ease, before it then collapsed under the combined weight of tiger and ox. Old Man and leaves and making them creak and crackle. Old Man Junpa walked ahead, with me following close behind, our rifles ready in our hands. Though it was nighttime, the tracks weren't difficult to make out because the ground was damp. When the moon clouded over, Old Man Junpa lit a torch and marched on, unyielding. Spooring a tiger at night with a lit torch—only madmen would do such a thing! The tiger could be crouched down hiding somewhere, and we were making it easy for it to spot us, for it to ambush us. When I pointed out as much, Old Man Junpa stopped and glowered at me, saying, "If you're scared, why don't you go home, put on your wife's sarong and keep it on for good." So I kept quiet, but I felt an immense relief every time he extinguished the torch. I still can't help but wonder to myself: what if Old Man Junpa hadn't been by my side that night? Probably I would have let the tiger take the ox and go. Probably I would have accepted my fate and the poor luck of losing Din and the dishonor of it. Probably I would have fixed the shed's fence, made it stronger, made it sturdier, made it taller (but how tall would have been enough?), and probably I would have had to buy a new ox, or lease a new one, or maybe I would have just taken my wife and my remaining three oxen back to Praeknamdang, abandoning our hut, abandoning the fields that we'd worked so hard to claim and clear, having to endure the ridicule of my neighbors: *Look at that lad Kwantien—what business did he have going to settle down in Nern Tago Dum, all the way in the wilderness like that? Then the minute a tiger shows up and makes meat out of just one of his oxen, he comes running back with his tail between his legs.* Old Man Junpa would never have allowed me to do such a thing, not as long as he walked this earth. But right then, his fury had driven him beyond sense. He was a proud man. He took pride in being a master tiger slayer, and he had his honor to defend. For four of the oxen would ultimately become its prey, but it had also been quick to settle on Din as the first. Presented with a herd, a tiger will study each animal carefully, and it'll always target the weakest one of them, the one that's crippled or wounded or deformed or very young or very old. From the moment it saw the tiger, perhaps perched on the fence, poor Din must have known it was the target. By the time it had breathed in the tiger's scent and heard the low snarl rising from within the tiger's throat, by the time it saw the tiger's fangs and claws and saw the tiger's shining, deep green eyes, its strength had already fled, its knees had probably gone weak and buckled as though struck by a curse. It would have been paralyzed by an ancient, primal fear passed down through the bloodline over tens or hundreds of thousands of years, from one generation of bovines to the next. I knew full well I was never going to see Din again in this life. Din was a jet-black ox, its coat shiny, with a white mark in the shape of a bodhi leaf in the middle of its brow, and white streaks on its switch. It was a lively steer with a slightly odd personality. On its first day learning to plow, it was resistant, and simply plopped itself down on the ground. When Garagade whipped it with a bamboo twig, it tucked its chin like it was about to charge at her, and I ended up having to give it several whacks. The second day, it ran off, refusing to be yoked, and then went for a leisurely stroll, grazing along the edge of the forest. By the time I tracked it down, I'd lost a lot of time, and again had to reprimand it. But it never got upset with me. It liked having its thighs—a handspan in length—scratched all the way around. Before it became stumpy-tailed, it would lord itself over the other oxen, throwing its weight around and acting as if it were the boss, horning the others, and if one of the other oxen did something to cause it displeasure, it challenged it to a fight right away. But after it lost its switch, it became humbler, even a little melancholy, and avoided fights, even avoided confrontations. It was still a young ox, not quite fully grown, but it nonetheless almost certainly weighed more than that son of a demon tiger, and yet its greater weight hadn't saved it. Quite likely, its neck had snapped right away, with a single clamp down of those sharp, powerful fangs. The moonlight was now dim, now bright. The tiger stopped from time to time and then, because it knew it was being pursued, pressed on and on, dragging its prey with ruthless determination. There were moments when we thought we'd possibly gotten within gunshot range. We'd see bushes quivering not far ahead, and we'd quicken our feet, but then it'd turn out that our eyes were playing tricks on us, or so it appeared. The tiger pushed on. It was downwind from us and so could pick up our scent, or perhaps at times it could see us, even in the dark. Its eyes were much keener than ours, and when our torch was lit, no doubt it would have been able to see us even more easily. Daybreak had arrived by the time we found Din's body, lying stiff on its side under a makha tree, its neck broken, its scruff showing the puncture marks of four massive fangs, its tongue hanging out of its mouth, its eyes bulging, frozen and lifeless, its shoulders and back slashed by the tiger's claws, the cuts looking as though they were made by razor blades, its belly mauled and ripped open, innards spilling out everywhere. The state of Din's carcass showed that son of a demon tiger had gorged in a rush, gorged in fear that it could be in danger itself. Though dawn's first light was still weak, an enormous army of green tree ants were already awake and all over Din's body like a rash, and the swarm of flies over its body kept growing and growing, the dark insects flying and hopping in a chaos of greediness. Shortly afterwards, a large colony of big-headed ants arrived and claimed Din's mouth and its eyelids. Old Man Junpa's call was to the drawn-out days and nights of Old Man Junpa's and my absence, she'd barely dared to step outside the hut, even during the daytime. She looked wan and frail, having neglected to eat and sleep. At night, she'd kept the oil lamp burning bright through all the dark hours, hours that had seemed interminable. She was tipped off right away, by our silence, that Din was dead while its murderer still roamed free. The remaining three oxen looked all the more wretched. They made a lot of noise greeting Old Man Junpa and me. They were happy to see we'd returned, but contained within their greeting calls were also echoes of their questions, their asking us for news: *Was your hunt for the tiger successful? But where was our friend Din?* They all looked half-starved, having been neglected by Garagade, and looked like they needed water. They were scared, worried, and sad—the way they carried themselves told me so, the noises they made told me so, and the look in their eyes told me so. In the cattle shed, they all came and gathered around me, sighed, and rested their chins on my shoulders. Each one of them was full of grim, weighty thoughts that they wanted to share and express. I was no less gloomy, and no less upset, than they, but I forced myself to carry on. That very evening, I reconstructed the shed's fence, making it even taller and sturdier, and I cut them grass and fetched them water. The following morning, I rose early, right when day broke, and went out to plow the fields as usual, yoking Lom and Fai together and using Naam as a substitute. Garagade also came out to the fields and helped by ripping out weeds and aroids and digging out tree roots a little here and there. She tried to behave normally, her face betraying nothing all morning. But a little past three in the afternoon, she simply stopped and swept her gaze all around herself, and the oxen, working only grudgingly anyway, likewise stopped and swept their gazes all around themselves, which and shrubs, the climbing and crawling vines, the plants with underground bulbs, and even the cogon grass, all seemed to harbor spirits and seemed drunk on the rain they were fed, to the point of mania. Where the land had yet to be tilled and converted into planting fields, grasses and creepers burgeoned. Subterranean bulbs and corms and tubers sprang leaves and even conspicuously flowered. Trees that had been hacked down to stumps, only ankle- or knee-high, developed fresh buds, which shot forth, spreading from a thumb in length to a handspan, from a handspan to a cubit. Wherever seeds lay, they pushed their roots into the ground, and new growth sprouted upwards, spreading from a thumb in height to a handspan, from a handspan to a cubit. The ebony tree on the knoll appeared to grow more massive and blacker, its limbs and leaves ever denser and more crowded. The hours of daylight seemed to dwindle and dwindle, while the nights were so full of darkness and silence. The assembly of the jungle's peculiar noises made our hair stand on end, and it seemed they would go on forever and ever. Right before our eyes, the jungle was reclaiming the land we had wrested from it. But I said to myself, "I'm not perturbed. Next year, I'll pour in even more labor, and I *will* expand my domain," and every morning I put my head down and carried on plowing and harrowing, and every afternoon I carried on the work of uprooting seedlings and transferring them to their new plots. Garagade, though scared, came out to the fields all the same, working alongside me all the while. Her belly had grown larger, and she experienced some morning sickness, as was to be expected, which, when its symptoms struck, made her have to stop and take a break, but she was always quick to resume work. As for Old Man Junpa, he grudgingly prepared our meals, but otherwise he was obsessed with the tiger. Every single day, he ventured into the forest with his rifle, disappearing for many hours at a to his shoulders, his gray beard and mustache were unkempt and scruffy, his fingernails and toenails were curled and filthy—his obsession had utterly possessed him. I turned away and tried to walk off, but he came after me, hounding me further. "This conversation isn't over," he said, and all I said back to him was, "Old Man Junpa, Father, you're drunk. Go and get some sleep." Though I knew he had been holding his tongue, his outburst unsettled me and filled my head with racing thoughts. I felt hot inside. I felt restless. That villain's appearance had changed everything. Before the attack, we used to head out at dawn to start tilling the land, but more and more these days, we held off until later, until the sun was well up in the sky. Before, we used to keep setting seedlings into the ground until dusk, until the sky was losing light, but these days, more and more, by mid-afternoon we would retreat from the fields. And Garagade had begun to lose heart. One night, sitting there hugging her knees, she confessed, "I want to go back to Praeknamdang. I don't want to give birth in the middle of the jungle, not with a tiger running around." Well, that hit me hard, because her child was my child, wasn't it? and I said, "If we're going to go back to Praeknamdang, we shouldn't delay it, not even for another day." Old Man Junpa promptly barked from somewhere over by the cattle shed, "Whoever wants to go back can go right ahead. I'm staying here in Nern Tago Dum, even if I have to do it by myself." Every day, the three oxen acted more and more skittish and frightened. After their day's work in the fields, they often refused to stay in their shed and instead tried to share the hut with us. Fai seemed the worst off: previously, it had been a laid-back, good-natured ox, mostly unperturbed when the others bumped or knocked into it; its main concern had been eating, and to it, everything was equally tasty, grass or leaves, tender or tough, and when it was allowed to rest, it no time to waste, and now Naam, judging from its gait, was going to be unable to work for days, three at least, and right away the colossal weight of my worries bore down on me. Oxen can gore each other crippled, and all I could do was pray that Naam wouldn't be so unfortunate. I led Lom out of the water, grabbed Fai's lead rope and dragged them both back to the cattle shed. I lashed Fai more than ten times with the end of its own rope, lashed it on the ear, where I knew it would smart, and it yelped and whined, all of a sudden afraid, and went weak-kneed as though it were looking at a tiger again. I returned to the stream, to fetch Naam and bring it back to the shed. But on the opposite side of the water, in the area where it'd last been standing, Naam was no longer anywhere to be seen. I swam across, climbed up the bank, and looked for its hoofprints and blood on the grass, which I found quickly. The trail it left led into the woods, and the signs were that it had staggered slowly along, directionless, a lonesome ox wandering in the wilderness. I followed the prints, and the bloody marks around them, which seemed to grow bigger and bigger and more intensely red, and a chill ran down my spine when I saw them joined by the paw prints of a tiger, which suddenly materialized on top of and among Naam's hoofprints. The prints came from a large tiger, with a limping left forefoot that didn't firmly meet the ground. There was no mistaking it—those prints belonged to the same monster that had taken Din! That son of a demon tiger had been circling us the whole time, taking stock, keeping watch, probably at times approaching, at other times retreating farther back. It had probably been spying on Old Man Junpa, Garagade, and me, and our three oxen and been waiting for opportunity to be on its side. I ventured deeper into the forest, following the tracks left by both ox and tiger. I contemplated calling out to Naam but decided against it. I stopped. I looked around. Everywhere, the surroundings were made up of nothing but silence and an anarchy of green, replete with uncanny danger. About a furlong away from the stream, Naam's hoofprints abruptly broke off. Where they ended, the prints showed its hoofs having stamped over and over again in the same place, and the tiger's paw prints, too, showed its paws having stamped over and over again in the same place, stepping right on top of the hoof marks again and again. The ground and the surrounding vegetation were splattered with blood, and beyond there was a wide impression of an ox's body laid on its side and dragged along the ground, surely by a tiger with its sharp fangs buried in the ox's neck, and there were scrape marks along the surface made by the ox's back toes and its hip, and pools of fly-swarmed blood. It was a terrible scene and, confronted with it, I knew what I needed to do. By the time I made it back to the hut, I was entirely composed. Calmly, and without embellishment, I recounted to Old Man Junpa and Garagade what had happened. I got my rifle and my possibles bag, into which I packed dried rice and grilled beef jerky. Old Man Junpa, swearing from the minute I finished my account, grabbed his rifle and possibles bag too. Garagade sank to sitting on the floor, ashen-faced, lips quivering, hands clasped over her swollen belly. I couldn't say anything further to her, and it was Old Man Junpa who found it within himself to at least say to Garagade, "You're going to have to stay home alone. Kwantien and I might be gone for some days," and then he picked up his bottle gourd, which had been filled with moonshine, took a swig from it, slapped the cork back on with a *thub*, and left the hut. He was giddy like a child. He was plainly pleased to see that, finally, I'd put my gun in my hands and was about to go out into the forest and hunt that heinous beast. I knew that, candidly, what Old Man Junpa had wanted to tell Garagade was: "Kwantien and I won't be back until we've slaughtered that son of a demon." Those was about two arm spans up from the ground, more than half of it already eaten. Nonetheless, I recognized those remains to be Naam, recognized the bell still tied to its neck, the bell now chiming in the morning's tender breeze. Tigers, given the time, will always drag their prey up to an elevated place, to safeguard it from scavengers on the ground. But even so, Naam's carcass hadn't been spared: a flock of about thirty vultures had stationed themselves around its body and were pecking away at it quietly, and without hurry. The ungodly stench of those massed birds nearly caused me to vomit. Old Man Junpa made the decision to continue following the tiger, rather than waiting by the carcass. Its tracks were pronounced given the softness of the rain-soaked soil and the increased weight of its body after a large meal. Its stride had shortened, indicating more of a relaxed stroll than anything, its route meandering through the understory of tall trees. There were times when its tracks left no doubt that it had plopped itself down on the ground and taken a break, completely nonchalant—maybe it had licked its lips, licked its paws, taken a short nap, woken up, stretched, before casually moving on. Maybe it had climbed a tree or two, perhaps to survey the jungle, perhaps just out of curiosity. It must have known we were following it, and the way it behaved amounted to nothing short of flaunting in our faces how it still roamed free. At one point, we came upon a large pile of its shit, still warm, a thin white cloud of condensation swimming around it, and came upon its piss— clear, glistening and pungent—left wet on leaves. We couldn't be far behind. Carnivores' shit and piss have a revolting and unholy smell; the shit and piss of herbivores don't have that same vile stench. From that spot, its paw prints ended at the side of a creek, where it had probably stopped for water before paddling leisurely across to the other side. In turn, we too crossed the creek, our bags *reeling back, and she was never able to get up again, no matter how I tried to bite or shake her. These monkeys are strange and funny but also dangerous. They're tender and delicious, though—and all it takes to make them stop moving is one light slap in the head. With them, all I need to watch out for are those red things that bring heat and light and their long, black sticks that can blast like thunder from afar. That's it, nothing else*—or something like that anyway. I believe their impression of us humans must be something along those lines, and it's not inaccurate. Why did that beast have a lame left forepaw? I reckon it got stabbed by a porcupine quill. Tigers love to eat porcupines, and there used to be a lot of them in the jungle. Contrary to the myth, a porcupine is no match for a tiger, not in the least. One smack by the tiger and the porcupine's dead. But the tiger's arrogance is what gets it into trouble. In attacking a porcupine, a tiger will sometimes be careless—its paw will get quilled, and become infected, and soon the tiger is no longer fast or deft enough to hunt boars, muntjacs, or other deer comfortably, and it will turn its sights instead to people's domestic animals like oxen and water buffaloes, and eventually it will turn to hunting humans. Why did that tiger suddenly appear at Nern Tago Dum? My first guess was that it had once had territory somewhere deep in the forest to the west, but after its injury, another tiger had come prowling onto its turf, and though it had attempted to put up a fight, it had been defeated and so fled east. Or maybe the fight had been not over territory, but over a tigress. That was my initial theory, but that day, as evening approached, I began to have doubts. It was plain to see that son of a demon wasn't afraid of people. It must have killed a person before, I thought. When someone gets killed by a tiger, sometimes the dead person's soul will be unable to accept its untimely death and, angry and vengeful, will enter the animal's body and possess it, turning the creature from a mere tiger into a sming. You all might wonder why and how such a thing happens. If you were a child of the jungle like me, you'd understand. The jungle is a curious place. The jungle tunes people's heads and hearts to a different key. I used to think that if my life were ended by a tiger, I too would possess the body of my killer. I wouldn't resist it: it would be an untimely death, I would die in shock and in agony; everything that belonged to me in the past, everything that I possess in the present, everything to be accorded to me in the future, all of it would be eradicated by that death, and my soul would be bitter and vindictive. No, I wouldn't resist. A desire to take revenge against the world would be born within me, and I'd possess the tiger, absolutely, and no one would be able to talk me out of it. That, at least, used to be my thinking when I was a young man, and I still harbored those thoughts later on from time to time, even while I was a monk on tudong. Stories of sming tigers are tales of yore. You aren't children of the jungle, you didn't grow up in the dark shadows of the jungle the way I did. When you hear stories like these, you think they're fiction, silly fairy tales. But I'm not like you. I think they could be true . . . A sming tiger transfiguring itself into the wife of the huntsman who was perched upon a machan waiting to shoot it, and when the huntsman climbed down from the machan to greet her, turning back into a tiger and biting him to death . . . Back when I was a young monk and still industrious about taking myself out on tudong, every jungle community I came across had stories like these, their own stories about sming tigers and their devilry. You're going to say that those stories can't be true, and that they have no basis in reason, which would be correct—but not everything in this world can be explained with reason. Anyway, those were the thoughts running through my mind as I trudged along behind Old when he returned he was even more stern and sullen. His whole body vibrated with frustration and displeasure. He lay down with his head pointed north, legs stretched toward the fire, and I lay down with my head pointed south, legs stretched toward the fire. Our rifles were loaded with fresh gunpowder and percussion caps, but we didn't have them cocked, and we'd removed our powder horns from around our necks and laid them aside. When darkness arrived, the jungle droned with the noises of crickets and cicadas and babbler birds. Early in the night, a flock of racket-tailed drongos could be heard brawling. Owls hooted loudly as they landed on the fig's branches and peered down at us with their ominous eyes. There were the sounds of flying lemurs flapping through the air as they skipped from one treetop to the next, shrilling eerily like those pret ghosts condemned to eternal hunger; tokay geckos croaking a low, haunting croak; palm civets screaming a repeated *yok-yok-yok, yokk, yokk, yokk,* sounding as crazed and anguished as tortured souls; and there was the sound of our fire crackling. I could never quite get used to the sound of the jungle at night. I lay looking at the weeping fig's cascading roots, supine with my whole body flat on the ground—that's the safest position to sleep in while in the jungle, so Old Man Junpa had taught me. Exhausted, I fell asleep in no time. When I woke up again, I saw Old Man Junpa sitting there drinking moonshine, chin propped on a knee, eyes staring into the flames and mouth muttering something. He looked much aged. He appeared drunk, as ever. There was an unspoken understanding between us that on a night hunt like this, if one of us was asleep, the other was to maintain a wakeful eye. I knew Old Man Junpa wanted to let me get my fill of sleep, and once he figured I'd rested enough, he'd wake me so I could keep watch and he could have his turn. And I started to drift off again, in the midst of the jungle's ancient noises, to drift off in the midst of the darkness and the jungle's ancient mysteries. How insignificant that menagerie of sounds was compared to the darkness, the mysteries, the noises, and the quiet inside my own mind—that was a truth I learned only after I became a veteran at the practice of tudong. The tudong journey is simply a journey into the unruly jungle of one's mind. But during those days and nights of hunting that heinous tiger, I hadn't yet discovered that truth. I couldn't tell you how long I'd been slumbering when I was ripped from my sleep by a wave of screams and wails, primal and agonized. The cries told of extreme fright and unbearable pain. It was a human voice, but that was no human language. Along with the screaming I heard a thunderous roar, one so forceful and so full of terror and savagery that it would have a set a stone quivering in fear. Our fire was much diminished, now reduced to embers and ash and wisps of tottering white smoke. The rain had lightened to a gray mist. I felt as though I'd woken into a nightmare. For a long moment—too long—I was too stunned to react. The fear, the confusion, the panic, the horror of what I was seeing—they were like a swarm of hornets bombarding me. In front of me, seen through the mist and a curtain of smoke, a large tiger stood next to our dying fire, its long, sharp fangs buried into the flesh above Old Man Junpa's right knee, and it was jerking and tossing its head in the most ruthless manner, intent on dragging Old Man Junpa away. But Old Man Junpa was tough and he was dogged, and he fought the tiger with every bit of life in him. With both hands, he hung on tight to the rooty ridges and ribs of the fig tree's trunk by his head, his strained, powerful arms shaking. His broad chest was expanded and heaving up and down. His mouth, agape, screamed and shrieked and swore. He kicked out with his left leg as hard as he could, over and over again, at the tiger's immense face. The evil seized its opportunity to turn hunter, and, commanded by its dark instinct, launched an offensive that was more abrupt and ruthless and horrific and blood-curdling than I could have anticipated. I must admit that, in the dim light cast by the dying fire, I never got a good, full look at it. I only saw parts of it at a time, in shapes and fragments, or in blurs when it moved. But my ears certainly heard its roars, and my heart certainly felt the terror it struck. That made it seem more like a nightmare than a living animal, but what it had done to Old Man Junpa was all too real and devastating. I pictured myself running hysterically to get away from that scene of horror, too panicked to care which way I was going, my sanity buckled under the weight of what I'd seen—running hysterically like I'd done when I found Mae Duangbulan minutes after her final moment. But, although it took everything in me, I willed myself to stay put. There Old Man Junpa lay, silent and motionless, apart from his chest, which still heaved up and down. His eyes were astonishingly tranquil, and still limpid. Knitted though his brows were, the rest of his face was smooth. His jaw was still clenched tight, so tight in fact that blood seeped out of the corners of his mouth without his knowing it. His right knee had been so badly bitten that his leg had nearly been severed in two. Scarlet blood flowed freely from the wound, with clots starting to form along the edges of it. It was the stillness and quietness of his eyes that helped me regain my wits. I wrapped his wound with his khao mah cloth, and one at a time and with great difficulty, I pried his hands open and removed them from the ridges and ribs of the weeping fig's trunk—it was with beyond-human grit that he'd hooked his hands onto the tree. His palms were badly cut, all ten of his fingernails blood-blackened, and his arms and torso were still stiff from the tension. I slung Ninlagaan and Sai Fah Faad over my left shoulder.

ingredients and heading into the jungle to find unusual herbs the way he used to. Draped over my right shoulder, he lay unstirring but warm. I knew there was still breath in him. Blood kept dribbling out of his wound, and out of the corners of his mouth; my clothes were soaked with it. But he made not a sound—he was a tough old bastard. I tried to reconstruct what had happened: Old Man Junpa had probably lain back, thinking he'd stretch his tired body out for a moment. He probably hadn't meant to sleep, but being exhausted and inebriated, he'd probably dozed off without first waking me up. That son of a demon had probably been lurking nearby, watching us, keeping its eyes trained on us in the dark while staying quiet, hidden, and had closed in on us when it saw the fire dying out and us sound asleep, the whole time considering the best approach and deliberating which one of us, Old Man Junpa or me, would make the more suitable prey. It had probably inched back when it saw either Old Man Junpa or me move, or perhaps when our fire had happened to flare up. Perhaps it had crouched down, hiding in the bushes. Perhaps it had climbed a nearby tree and perched atop one of its boughs, from where it had looked down on us. Likely, it had retreated and advanced several times. Perhaps it had come and stood over Old Man Junpa's sleeping body and sniffed. But it had been patient enough to back off again until it saw that the fire was much died down and no one was about to wake up. Then it had slunk over, coming very close, close enough to sniff my or Old Man Junpa's legs. But as long as we lay perfectly horizontal to the ground, prone or supine, it wouldn't be able to figure out where to leap in and bite, and it would grow flustered, its limited intelligence stumped. But as soon as someone's arm or leg or head revealed a propitious angle, it would swoop in and bite. It had probably watched humans sleep before, and had learned to stay still and there, because I had a degree of familiarity with that part of the jungle. Still, I staggered and stumbled along for a full five hours before I made it back to the hut, near the break of dawn. I heard wild chickens crowing and heard koel birds cawing and saw pinkish-gray light rising from the horizon over the eastern edge of the forest as I rasped out a call to Garagade, and I can still see, in my mind's eye, the state she was in when she opened the hut's door and came out to meet me, smoking lamp in hand and paper umbrella spread over her head: her face was markedly pale and her eyes red-rimmed and dry—she had clearly spent the night sleepless, worrying herself sick and ragged in our absence. She'd been left a prisoner in the hut. My arrival meant freedom, and she beamed at the prospect of her liberation. But then she saw Old Man Junpa, and her face dropped. She was startled and became unsteady on her feet. But she saved her questions and didn't begin asking what, where, when, how. Instead, she squeezed her lips together, set her jaw, and hurried off to start a fire so she could boil water right away. By the time I lay Old Man Junpa down on the bed in his room, his breathing had grown exceedingly feeble. The blood from his wound had dried and hardened onto the khao mah cloth I'd wrapped around it, and the blood from the corners of his mouth had dried into crusts running up his cheeks. His face was pallid and his body was slack, but his eyes remained clear. Garagade came in to help dress the wounds. She cleaned the blood off and dabbed the sides of the wounds with a clean rag she'd dampened with warm water, and then she ground up a nutgall and sprinkled the powder onto the cuts to help the flesh reseal itself faster. His right knee was so gruesome I couldn't bear to look at it. The tiger's fangs had pierced all the way down to the bone, which had been broken by the clamp of its jaws, and both of his legs had been clawed by the tiger, with places where the bone again, and Garagade would have had to stay and watch the hut alone once again. In that moment, I was beyond spent. Really, what I longed to do more than anything was to sleep for a long time, but given the circumstances, I had to keep my eyes open. There was no other choice: I had to bury Old Man Junpa there in Nern Tago Dum. But first I had to build him a casket, and I was going to make it the sturdiest, most neatly built casket possible, I would make sure it was the perfect size, the right proportions, I would dowel it tight and tidy. I was a decent carpenter, and we had plenty of lai bamboo already sawed up and piled. We had knives, machetes, and axes on hand. Old Man Junpa would rest comfortably, I would make sure of it. And once I had his coffin built, my next task would be to dig him a grave—three cubits wide, three cubits deep, and six cubits long. (Or was three cubits deep enough? I wondered.) I would point his head west, the cardinal direction of the dead. Though it was going to be a funeral deprived of religious rites, it would not be deprived of the decency of tradition. I didn't cry at all; I was numb, and weak from exhaustion. But I couldn't afford to sit and sulk— there was too much to be done. Ought I to join Old Man Junpa's hands over his chest? And ought he to have flowers and a candle and joss sticks in his hands so held? The eucharis lilies and blood lilies he'd planted along the perimeter of our front yard were in bloom. I was about to call out, *Garagade, I want Old Man Junpa to have some flowers. Could you help pick me a bunch?* when I heard her calling out to me. Her voice, weak and hoarse, trembled as though she were cold to the core. I went out through the door of the hut, to find her in the front yard, in the middle of the blurring rain, the ground beneath her feet wet and black and strewn over with wilted sarapi petals, the sky above her low and black and full of roiling clouds. Garagade didn't utter a word, she merely pointed down at the ground by her feet and held her finger frozen. My eyes went to the spot. There, I saw the paw prints of a large tiger, one with a hobbling left forefoot that didn't press firmly into the ground. Given their state—crisp and fresh—it was mere moments ago that that son of a demon had been right here, stepping right into our territory! Its trail went around by the hut and by the cattle shed; I followed its steps. I saw my own footprints from when I had staggered out of the jungle, which were deep and distinct because of Old Man Junpa's weight added to mine, and I saw the tiger's paw prints trailing right behind. A chill ran down my spine. My skin was suddenly covered in goosebumps. Without my having noticed, the beast had stalked me all of last night, hungry, seeking revenge. I'd dared to snatch its prey straight from its mouth. I'd assaulted it with a smoldering log. How many times while I trudged and wove through the jungle straining to carry Old Man Junpa, off guard and defenseless, had it considered attacking me? What had given it a faint heart? What had made it hold back? Regardless, it'd stayed on my heels the whole time. That first taste of Old Man Junpa's blood had probably only made it thirst for more, probably its craving had nearly driven it mad, and so it'd followed me all the way back to the hut with unbridled audacity. It had probably looked through the slits in our bamboo walls and observed us, and had then looped around the cattle shed, eyeing the oxen through the fence, and it'd probably thought to itself, *Not uninteresting, but it's not yet time for that. The truth is, I eat men. They're dangerous, but there's no prey more delectable, and I already let one slip away last night. Let me eat all the humans first, oxen. Then your turn shall come.* Last night, it'd probably fixed upon Old Man Junpa, and the reason it had followed me was to reclaim its prey and take it back. Nothing in the world was going to deter it or change its mind. But it was light out now, and with the

the air with a stench like rotting feces—these plants bring bad luck, they're an ill omen. Beyond the fields lay the dark, damp wilderness that surrounded us in all directions, bursting with power and life and readying itself to expel us from the land. My father's body, my hut, my wife, my oxen, the land of my livelihood, and I myself, were hemmed in by that uncanniness and solitude. We stood out like something alien, something out of place, something at odds and incongruous with all that circumscribed us. In the still-misting rain, butterflies and dragonflies were out flying. A swarm of winged weaver ants moved languidly through the air, while on the ground an army of them was busy migrating from one nest to another, taking eggs and food. White-rumped shamas chirped, their song at once sweet and spirited. I considered everything all around me. I thought about whether to flee or fight. I knew that whatever my decision, I needed to act. I'd poured so much into this place, so had Old Man Junpa and Garagade. How could I abandon everything we had built? No, I was going to pursue that hellish demon to the end of this earth. It might be a man-eating tiger, it might be a sming tiger—cunning and uncommonly cruel—but sooner or later I was going to defeat it. At least for now it'd taken cover in the jungle. As soon as I'd buried Old Man Junpa, I'd go after it. I didn't have time to build my father a coffin; I would have to bury him in whatever way I could. I grabbed a hoe and headed towards the knoll where the big ebony stood, at the western limit of our land, and there I set about digging Old Man Junpa's grave. Long ago, he'd once told me to aspire to be like the ebonies, miraculously tough trees. Known among herbalists as the black elephant king, ebony has bark that is used as an ingredient in elixirs of life. Their limbs or trunks might split or break or crack if struck by lightning or burned, but given rain, they will always produce new buds. Their roots, too, are stronger and run deeper than when Garagade was coming out. The emptiness at the center of her was more pronounced than ever, her eyes dull and distant and her face even more pallid. Draped over her forearm were a black sarong and a fresh black blouse, and in her hand she held a coconut shell, raven-black, which was her water scoop, a bar of soap she boiled up herself, and two charred makrut limes for washing her hair. She was headed to the dock to bathe; there was no further role for her in the funereal rites. Now it was my turn to say goodbye to Old Man Junpa, to ask him for forgiveness for all the ways I'd wronged him in my life, and to wish his soul a safe passage to a better place. Now it was time, I found it unendurably hard. It was so difficult for me to let go of him because I became orphaned of a mother at ten, and he'd been both my father and mother ever since. I remember that I was already nearly twelve and every day he still made me a break-fast of rice broth sweetened with sugarcane juice. He was the one who taught me how to write my กขฃs, and how to add and sub-tract, before putting me under the tutelage of Luang Paw Kom, the abbot of Praeknamdang Temple, so that I could study Khmer. The entire time I was a temple boy, he would never go long without a visit. I remember once I couldn't pass urine, and he fed me grilled sugarcane. One time, I had scald head, and he ground up a jew-el-orchid root and sprinkled the powder on my lesions for me. Once, I got unlucky and was bitten in the calf by a maewsao viper, and nearly died. My heart felt like it was wobbling in my chest, and my vision was blurred, and I was in pain and very drowsy, and I thought I was in the middle of a clearing that spread as far as the eyes could reach, and all I saw were dying thickets, dying shrubs, and a snag with a morose flock of crows sitting on its branches, and the wind whistled, and I heard somebody's voice calling my name from a distance, and, powerless to resist, I answered that call, which prompted Old Man Junpa to jump into action, mashing up hop-head leaves and mixing the liquid from them with rice whiskey, and pouring the concoction down my throat, and he called my name again and again to keep me from falling asleep, and he certainly saved my life that day. He was the one, too, who taught me how to cook, how to boil rice and make different viands. Once, when I was eleven, he smacked me so many times we both lost count, because he'd bought me a hunting knife, and I, in a fit of childish aggression, used it to hack his patch of homalomenas to shreds. One time, when I was fourteen or fifteen, I was trekking through the jungle with him and I tried to shoot a rogue boar with tusks three knuckles long, but my aim was off—the bullet only grazed its back. The boar dropped its chin and charged at me, and I'd quite likely be dead now if he hadn't fired Ninlagaan and stopped the animal in its tracks. In my whole life, I've known few people the way I knew him. When it came time for us to part, I was heartsick with grief. I knew that he had a sizable black mole at the base of his neck, which, they say, is a mark of misfortune, because the owner of such a mole is doomed never to find peace and comfort. I knew that he had chronic jungle fever which, no matter the treatment, he couldn't cure, and that he was laid up in bed groaning and shivering almost every time there was an extended stretch of rainy days and the air was cold and raw, and his symptoms were only alleviated when he gulped down large quantities of his medicinal spirits, made from his own special recipe. I knew that, really, deep down in his heart, he'd begun to grow dissatisfied with life as a hunter and having to collect things from the forest to sell, because the townsfolk at the market, who often gave him a condescending look or stared at him with a mixture of curiosity and pity, never offered him a fair price for his wares. It was a struggle to make ends meet, and he would hut, I joined my palms in front of my face and bowed my head at Old Man Junpa's feet, which became wet from my tears. I wanted for words. I didn't know what to say to him. I left the hut. Outside, the morning sun had dimmed, and dark, dense clouds had taken over the sky. A cool breeze moved in from the southwest, while a rumble sounded in the distance. The jungle seemed to be holding its breath in apprehension. Not a sound came from the birds or the wild chickens or the squirrels. I saw a pair of white-rumped shamas perched dead still on a tangle of vines. A large turtle waddling across the front yard stopped, and, as if anticipating something, retracted its head and legs into its shell. A sense of foreboding came over me because of the suddenness of the silence. Only the two oxen in the cattle shed huffed loud breaths and strained on the tethers tying them to a rail. Garagade was taking an awfully long time to bathe. I marched straight towards our dock, which was tucked between dense growths of pandans and torch gingers. There she was, in the shadow of the great rubber tree, perched on the ladder leading into the water, still as a statue. Her black sarong, wrapped over her bosom, shone from the water it had soaked up. The plane of her back, her shoulders with their gentle slopes, her trim, graceful arms: all were sublime and immaculate, but, after all she'd done and been through, and with her being pregnant, she looked more vulnerable and more delicate than ever. Her hair, which reached halfway down her back when loose, was dripping wet and collected into a topknot. Inside the coconut shell, her right hand squeezed the charred makrut limes, pressing out a blend of juice and pulp, and the refreshing scent wafted across to me. She bowed her head as she readied to pour the mixture over her gathered strands, her eyes shut tight. The stream was deep, its flow rapid, its water an opaque white. During that season, it was nearly three arm spans across. On the opposite bank were

156

swollen and marked with soot, and its mouth and jaw were still crusted with Old Man Junpa's blood. It glowered at me—it must have recognized me. I, too, glowered at it. And when it swaggered along the side of the stream, tossing glances at me, I too swaggered along my side of the stream, tossing glances at it. When it lowered its chest and crept close to the ground, I got down and lowered mine and crept close to the ground. When it grunted, I grunted. When it feinted to leap at me, I too feinted to leap at it. It puffed its chest out, raised its head high, and delivered a deafening roar. Then I, too, puffed my chest out, raised my head high, and delivered a deafening roar of my own, which took it by surprise. After that, it and I traded long stares, before it slowly walked away and disappeared between bushes below a tall and uneven overstory, still full of fury, of vindictiveness, of thirst for blood. Garagade looked over at me, and it was as if she didn't recognize me. I barely recognized myself in that moment. After waiting for Garagade to finish bathing so I could escort her back to the hut, I snatched up Sai Fah Faad, emptied out the old cap and gunpowder and loaded in a fresh set, opting for a ten-saleung lead cap, a heavy bullet I rarely used. I carried Old Man Junpa's body in my arms and walked straight from the hut to the grave I'd dug for him on the ebony knoll. I wasn't going to bury him yet, however. His body was stiff and cold to the touch; his mouth was frozen agape, his eyes trapped wide. I lowered him vertically into the grave, which made it appear as though he were standing with his legs sunken into the ground. I faced him west. A burst of wind lifted his grizzled hair, flapping it about. There was a white butterfly flitting by his head, and eventually it settled on his locks. I left him there. I walked past our front yard, crossed the stream, and climbed up onto the opposite bank, where mere moments ago, that son of a demon tiger had faced off with me. I looked for its paw probably come and stationed itself on this branch more than once, watching every move made by my father, my wife, my oxen, and me. It was stronger than us, and faster; its fangs and claws meant death. Its senses—sight, hearing, smell—were all sharper. But what scared me above all else was its extraordinary willpower. It must be a sming tiger! No doubt it was possessed by an evil soul! Regardless, I was undeterred, and thought, *You've spotted Old Man Junpa's body, haven't you, you fetid ghoul? Yours to claim, isn't that right? You've tasted the blood from that body, have you not? Rich and sweet, wasn't it, and moreish? Old Man Junpa's body is waiting for you under the ebony tree—go ahead, go get him. But I'll make you pay the price!* I climbed back down, looking for the tiger's next steps. As predicted, it'd spotted Old Man Junpa's corpse: its paw prints led south, trampling through thickets of weeds and cogon grass—straight towards the ebony tree. I tightened my grip on my rifle and leaned over it as I walked, my eyes darting left and right. I quickened my steps while keeping light and quiet on my feet. Once back within the limits of my property, it was no effort at all to identify its tracks, fresh on the ground, and soon it was in sight, creeping among the cogon grass. I saw it stop at times and raise its head high, sniffing for anomalous smells. It climbed the knoll from the west, and at the top it came directly face to face with Old Man Junpa. It paused, hanging back, but not for a second did its eyes ever let go of his corpse. I hunched low, and without a sound I went around the knoll to position myself east. I was behind Old Man Junpa's body, and I could see the tiger's face straight on. For a second it appeared to have picked up my scent, or perhaps the sound of a movement, and it stiffened, and looked as though it might retreat. The monsoon wind continued to drift in from the southwest. The sun blazed one minute and vanished the next. Gray clouds still hung in thick clusters, and the rain kept softly drizzling. It could have been such an ordinary rainy-season morning. I huddled behind a tangle of vines, my rifle pressed on my shoulder with the hammer cocked wide and ready, my pointer finger joined to the trigger. I knew the cap would do its job and the gunpowder its, and Sai Fah Faad wouldn't let me down. The beast walked straight towards Old Man Junpa's corpse, getting within seven or eight steps of him, before again halting, confused and uncertain. Perhaps it had expected its prey's blood to have a gamier smell; perhaps its nose had detected the foreign scents of ground turmeric and marl powder. It stared hard at Old Man Junpa's body. Yes, this was it, the prey it'd let slip away last night . . . but somehow altered. Something was off. It hesitated. It looked ready to depart. But then again, it was desperately famished. From its body language, you could tell it was infuriated and impatient for blood. It crouched down, and catching me completely off guard, roared at the top of its lungs, a roar mightier and more crazed than any other before, the forcefulness enough to make my heart jump out of my chest, make my hands and feet go weak and my bones feel like wax licked by fire. I needed every last bit of self-control to stop myself from screaming out in fear. The roar seemed to feed its wrath and desire for blood even further, and the next thing I knew, it launched itself at Old Man Junpa's corpse, its front paws spread wide to display claws held erect, its maw stretched wide to display fangs long and sharp, the cavity of its open mouth dripping with the clear, stringy saliva of its hunger. I rose to my full height. I pulled the trigger, and the kick of the gun sent me stumbling back two or three steps. The bullet—those ten saleungs of justice—entered it mid-chest, meeting its body a mere arm's length away from Old Man Junpa's corpse. On impact, it dropped straight down onto the side of the grave, but it didn't die nonsensically while asleep. She developed an aversion to light. Especially with her belly growing larger, her symptoms worried me. At night, she was wide-eyed and wired. She breathed loudly and constantly tossed and turned. She paced back and forth inside and outside, around the hut, and often went and did the same over by the cattle shed. At other times she was given to sitting completely motionless, staring at me for long stretches, apparently unaware she was doing it. I didn't know what else to blame but the horrific trauma she'd endured, on top of her pregnancy—or perhaps it was simply the jungle climate, its humid heat and humid chill alike. I nursed her as best I could, being myself unwell, down with a fever one day, better the next. Time and again, she raved on confusedly: she said that evil plague of a tiger was a sming, that it'd killed and eaten several people before and that it was possessed by a brutish and wicked soul, and she said it was still alive. With solemnity, she said she continued to see it, both in the day and at night. She saw it looking forlorn, walking alongside the stream and then rather somberly hanging its tongue out to lap up water. She saw it lying prone and still in the front yard in the middle of the rain. She saw it standing under the ebony tree, peering pensively into the sky at eventide. She saw it wander into the hut, go into Old Man Junpa's room, go into the kitchen, come into our room, where it stared at us with vindictive eyes. I thought she was simply having fever dreams and nightmares. I myself was hardly the picture of health: my breath felt hot, my limbs weak and heavy, I felt pain in my bones, my eyes were blurry, and I saw all kinds of things in doubles and triples, I had an unpleasant taste in my mouth and my tongue was dull to flavor. Still, I needed to build a new fence, and so I forced myself to get out of bed and chop bamboo to make posts, which I drove into the ground around the hut, tightly lined up together. I also wove a bamboo frame for the hut's roof and secured the windows with slats of hardwood. I outfitted the door with a new set of brackets and a new bolt. And, allowing myself no rest or delay after that, I resumed tilling the land. I had my heart set on getting fifteen rais planted this year, and I was determined to make it happen. Grass and other weeds had grown thick. I plowed the fields roughly over in one direction and plowed again across, feeling bitter throughout. I raked the harrow over the land until the grasses were mush. I dug out tree roots by the armful. I pulled seedlings from the nursery and right away set them into their new plots. When the harvest season arrived, I'd likely be doing the reaping by myself, because by the first month of the coming year, Garagade would probably give birth, and I'd have to bring her back to Praeknamdang for the delivery, and next summer it would be high time for me to build a house, and for that I'd probably have to go back down to Praeknamdang and ask friends and neighbors for help, and I ought to buy two more oxen as well. I'd need money for all this, so I'd better have rice on hand to sell or barter with. And I thought about my baby: was it going to be a boy or a girl? Who was it going to look like? Was it still healthy and strong, with Garagade being so frail? I was bone-tired, and almost ten plots of the paddy land had yet to be tilled, each one of them more than half a rai, and all that with only two oxen left to work with. I rose as soon as day broke and never made it back to the hut before nightfall. Then, I'd still have dinner to prepare and a sick wife to worry about. Both Lom and Fai were so skinny their ribs were showing in whole racks; the poor things were being worked to death. Their shoulders were battered and cut up from the constant pressure of the yoke. They hardly got to eat fresh grass, let alone monkeypod leaves and Manila tamarind shoots—I couldn't spare the time to pick these things for paddy fields—I was a vicious tiger, jealous of its territory. I was prepared to fight any invader onto my land, be they man of any name or beast of any kind. At the same time, though, it saddened me to have turned into a tiger, and irrevocably so, and I mourned deeply and yearned for my life as a human—but then I woke in a start. Yet even out of my slumber, I would lapse into thinking I'd woken up as a tiger. Deep one night, when the sky was clear, bright moonlight slipped in through the seams in the hut's walls, casting dark shadows across my chest and arms, which were pale and yellowish, and I nearly died from shock as I thought myself metamorphosed into a tiger while lying in my bed. When my fever improved somewhat, I went to check on the rice fields and was astonished: the parts of the land that I thought had yet to be tilled showed signs of having been plowed, even if not completely, not every plot. It must have been Garagade, worried about our paddies, worried about our progress, not wanting me to shoulder the burden alone and trying to lighten my load. Lom and Fai looked even gaunter and more undernourished. Their shoulders now had deep split wounds, they had constant tears streaming out of their eyes, and they were swarmed all over by fruit flies. They looked like they'd been worked without any rest at all. Sometimes I woke up and noticed that Garagade wasn't inside the hut, but I was always too groggy to go and find her, and I simply assumed she'd gone to have a sit outside, under the sarapi tree in front of the hut, where we had the bamboo daybed. On the twelfth night of the waxing moon in the eighth month of 2437 BE, I woke up in the dark and lay awake, my mind wandering far and wide, and I couldn't fall back asleep. I left the hut, intending to go and keep Garagade company under the sarapi tree—but she wasn't there. Then I saw, to my surprise, that Lom and Fai weren't to be found in their shed, and my mind flew to the place I least wanted it to go: the tiger! But how could it be? That infernal beast was dead. I'd slain it with my own bullet. Or was this another tiger? Hidden behind a billow of clouds, the twelve-night-old moon was but dim. The air, meanwhile, was full of the scent of nocturnal flowers. I grabbed Old Man Junpa's trident from the space below the roof above the hut's door and wrapped my hands tight around it. I wasn't fearful at all. Having vanquished that heinous tiger, I thought nothing in this life—man, beast, or even spirit—could ever scare me again. I walked all the way out to the edge of our front yard, and peering out into the fields, I saw there my two oxen yoked and being forced to draw the harrow, and I thought, ah, so Garagade's taken them out. So worried was she about me and about our farm, she was out there with the harrow, pushing to have the tilling done and behind us, even if it was halfway into the night and she was sick and pregnant. I walked closer. And then I gripped the trident hard: in the murky light of the moon, the figure rocking the harrow, its feet pumping the frame, was not Garagade but a large tiger, perhaps twelve cubits long from head to tail, its left grip on the harrow's handlebar loose and ungainly. I blinked. I stared hard. Yes, indeed, it *was* that son of a demon tiger from hell. I charged at it. I lifted the trident over my head and launched it as hard as I could. The iron of the three-pronged spear rammed deep into the middle of its back. It turned and looked at me for a second, before howling out a tortured cry that sent a chill echoing through the forest. Then it ran, hobbling off into the dim of the night. I detached the harrow and unyoked Lom and Fai. I brought my oxen back to their shed, all the while with my heart still pounding inside my chest and the hair on my skin standing on end. I wasn't dreaming. But dream or reality, I knew from that night forward I must absolutely forbid Garagade

# AFTERWORD

It would seem, once again, that the work itself has taken enough of the reader's time and any sort of an afterword should be unnecessary. But in this case, foregoing such a note would constitute a literary sin. For accounts of how Thais of eras past endeavored to use reason to explain various natural phenomena, my source was Chaophraya Thiphakorawong's *Jodmai Het* (also known as *Nangsue Sadaeng Kijjanukij*). This book serves as a testament to how people in times prior to the legislation of the Compulsory Primary Education Act also had their own ways of seeking knowledge. For information about the uses of medicinal herbs, my source was a folding-book manuscript (samut khoi) whose author, scribe, and date of transcription were not given. However, those with some knowledge of medicinal herbs are likely already aware that nutgalls are an excellent antihemorrhagic; that taguay, besides its fruit being a treatment for worms in ungulates, can also help alleviate sinus symptoms when its dried leaves are rolled and smoked; and that the jewel orchid works like magic to relieve itching.

For stories about mysteries of the jungle and its fauna as they relate to beliefs in the supernatural, my sources and inspirations were many. Of them, those that I must acknowledge are: *Nitan Borankadi* by Prince Damrong Rajanubhab, in particular the chapter "Seua Yai Nai Muang Chumphon"; *Kampi Saiyasat Chabab Somboon* by the astrologer known as Yanchote, an immensely interesting tome from a parapsychological perspective; *Pra Putta Jao Luang Niyom Prai* by Chali Iamkrasin, which, at the very least, provided me with a clear picture of jungle environments in Thailand during the reign of King Rama V; documentaries about tigers, by National Geographic in particular; and articles about the lives of animals by Sangkhit Chanthanaphot that were published in *Fah Muang Tong* magazine around 1976, combined with folklore about Thailand's jungles (which surely must exist in every jungle community), especially that from the villages deep in the forests of Khonburi District, Nakhon Ratchasima Province. I had lived among the locals of that area for quite some time, when I stayed with Teerayut Daojunteuk,[1] the author of the novel *Chabon*. There still remained, after what Teerayut had written into that novel, a trove of folk legends and an assortment of other tales about the jungle—legends and tales that, if woven and arranged and given shape, could, I thought, be turned into another novel. For accounts of life on tudong, my source was T. Liangpiboon's *Tudong Kawat*. For descriptions of crocodile hunting, my source was Phanom Tian's *Petch Phra Uma*.

For accounts surrounding King Rama V's cause of death, my source was Captain Sawat Juntanee's *Nitan Chao Rai*. I can no longer recall from where or whom I read or heard about Krom Luang Chumphon Khet Udomsak's indignation and show of strong will upon the French's occupation of the provinces of Chanthaburi and Trat. I also can no longer recall from where or whom I read or heard the early social science statistics giving the names of the people most well known in Thailand during the reign of King

---

1. Name transliterated phonetically, as no official or common English spelling could be found.

Rama V. For the deranged and barbaric method of torture I had Old Man Junpa use on the tiger that kills his wife, I was inspired by the novel *Torture Garden* by the French writer Octave Mirbeau. For the story Luang Paw Tien tells about a man transforming himself into a tiger to avenge his father's death, I was inspired by a tale of the supernatural in the book *Strange Tales from a Chinese Studio* by the Chinese writer Pu Songling. As for Garagade's final moment, those familiar with the story of Pentheus and Agave from Greek mythology will probably not have been surprised by it at all.

Both consciously and not, I had probably been thinking about those peculiar, timeworn tales since the time I was staying at Teerayut Daojunteuk's faded little hut on the Mun River, and then, twenty years later and unexpectedly, I found myself putting those stories on paper. One day in early 2002, I had set out to write a short story, which was meant to be a very short story. What I had had in mind was a ghost story precisely of the kind often subject to ridicule. But after two paragraphs, *The Understory* began to take shape. The story that I had started had shifted toward a new direction, and I, considerably irritated and discouraged, submitted to it, watched it from afar, to see how it would unfold. As things turned out, the very short story I had put myself to the task of writing remains yet to be written, and as things turned out instead, I wrote *The Understory*, which seems to have been born out of happenstance.

Respectfully,

Saneh Sangsuk

Victor's Hut, April 2002

**Saneh Sangsuk** is an award-winning Thai author who wrote *White Shadow* (2001) and the short story "Venom" (2001). In 2008, he received the Ordre des Arts et des Lettres (Order of Arts and Letters) Medal from the French Ministry of Culture for his remarkable contributions to literature. His works have been translated into seven different languages including English, German, French and Spanish. *White Shadow* is considered one of the best twenty novels in Thailand. Currently, he lives in Phetchaburi, Thailand.

**Mui Poopoksakul** is a lawyer-turned-translator with a special interest in contemporary Thai literature. She was awarded a PEN/ Heim Translation Fund grant for her translation of Saneh Sangsuk's *The Understory*. Mui's other translations include three story collections: *The Sad Part Was* and *Moving Parts*, both by Prabda Yoon, and *Arid Dreams* by Duanwad Pimwana. She is also the translator of Pimwana's novel *Bright* and has contributed widely to literary journals since she began her translation career. A native of Bangkok who spent two decades in the US, she now lives in Berlin, Germany.